Nigel gave her a quick glance. 'How far is it to the Well?'

'Only a mile or so. Actually, it was a baptistry, but the roof has disappeared. It's a holy well and once upon a time it was as famous as Lourdes.'

'What with wishes coming true and ills being cured all by magic we've got it made. I take it if you live in Cornwall you live happily and healthily for evermore. Tough on the undertakers,' Nigel smiled.

'And on doctors,' Emma grinned. 'Stand with your back to the Well, throw the pin over your left shoulder and wish. Be sure you don't say what you're wishing for.'

His eyes were warm and tender as they gazed down at her. 'Aren't you going to wish?'

Oh, yes, she had wished from the bottom of her heart that this might be the first of many such outings.

'Thank you so much for a lovely morning. I hope you enjoyed it too.'

Nigel's eyes sparkled with laughter and he leaned towards her and kissed her lightly on the cheek. 'I will have done if my wish comes true.'

Rhona Trezise was brought up in Cornwall. On her marriage to an architect she moved to London where they had a son and daughter. In 1967 she started writing short stories for women's magazines and the BBC, as well as picture scripts for teenagers and articles for educational journals. Having spent some time as a patient in various hospitals, she was so impressed by the loving care and charm of the nurses and doctors that she was prompted to weave romances around them. She obtains her medical information from many friends in the profession and from textbooks and medical journals.

Nurse Emma in Love is Rhona Trezise's tenth Doctor Nurse Romance. Recent titles include *Nurse in the Sun, The Children's Doctor* and *Nurse Palmer's Choice*.

NURSE EMMA
IN LOVE

BY

RHONA TREZISE

MILLS & BOON LIMITED
ETON HOUSE   18-24 PARADISE ROAD
RICHMOND   SURREY   TW9 1SR

*First published in Great Britain 1988
by Mills & Boon Limited*

© Rhona Trezise 1988

*Australian copyright 1988
Philippine copyright 1988
This edition 1989*

ISBN 0 263 76334 X

*Set in English Times 10 on 10½ pt.
03 – 8902 – 53519*

Typeset in Great Britain by JCL Graphics, Bristol

Made and Printed in Great Britain

CHAPTER ONE

'FOR PITY'S SAKE, not again, Nurse Glover!' Sister Darling's voice which could be so sweet when she was talking to doctors was taut with exasperation.

Emma looked into the Sister's steely grey eyes with equal indignation. Anyone would think she'd asked for the moon instead of merely for her weekend duty to be changed so that she could go home to Cornwall before the half-price travel offer on the soap powder tops she had collected from friends and relations was out of date.

She opened her mouth to reply, but Pamela Darling continued relentlessly,

'Whatever led you to believe you might be the answer to a sick patient's prayer? I'd like to know what made you leave your precious home town, since you're always anxious to get back there.'

Emma had only recently come to work on Sister Darling's ward. Before that she had had no difficulty at all in getting the Sister to oblige her in this way, but Pamela Darling seemed to have taken a dislike to her from the start.

'I'm not asking for time off, only for it to be changed, Sister. Nurse Keating doesn't mind changing,' Emma said, trying to sound suitably submissive.

The Sister gave a sweeping dismissive gesture. 'Get back to your work. You can change duties this time—but don't think you can make a habit of it, because you can't. My rotas don't make themselves, you know. I have other things to do than change them around for your benefit.'

5

'Thank you, sister.'

Emma hurried to the linen room which adjoined the Sister's office, her normally pink cheeks red with annoyance. She grasped a handful of her chestnut-coloured hair and tugged at it in frustration while she glared ferociously at a harmless bag which hung on the wall, with her large brown eyes.

'I hate you, you miserable——'

She heard the Sister's door open and froze. Was she going to come in here? Then it closed again and there was the sound of voices. So Dr Shaw had arrived for his morning session with her. Emma had wondered what they talked about. It certainly wasn't only work, for she heard their laughter, and when Sister Darling came from the room she would often look happy and flushed. Emma gave an ironic smile. Sister Darling's voice and manner would change now all right!

Nigel Shaw was the best-looking doctor in the hospital—and didn't he know it. He had straight fair hair with a wayward strand that fell over his forehead, which he would push back absent-mindedly with a well-manicured hand. Emma bet he practised that in front of a mirror. Unashamedly she went right up to the wall to hear what they were saying. She should have remembered listeners don't hear good themselves.

His low, seductive voice fascinated her and at first she just listened to its rise and fall without taking in the words. Then she heard him say,

'And why is there a scowl on that pretty face?'

Sister Darling's voice, despite its sugar-coating, sounded irritated.

'Give me strength, Nigel. That—that wretched student will drive me crazy!'

Emma scowled. The stupid woman, what was she talking about?

Dr Shaw chuckled. 'Hold on a minute, Darling. Which student is this?'

'Which student?' Her voice rose. 'Need you ask! It's that dopey rustic from Cornwall, Glover. God knows why she decided to go in for nursing—half the time she lives in another world peopled by pixies and pasties, I shouldn't wonder, and the other half she's wanting to scuttle back home. I wish to goodness she'd go there and stay there.'

'Oh, *that* child. Come now, Darling, is she so hopeless?' His voice was gently teasing.

It seemed to annoy her. 'A child, you call her! She's in her third year, although you'd never guess. She should have stayed in her beloved Cornwall, married some farmer's lad and had a brood of kids.'

Emma's eyes blazed. You know what I'd like to do to you, she thought furiously, and gave the unoffending bag which held pads and plastic sheeting a hefty thump. To her dismay there was also something hard and heavy in the bag, and it swung against the intervening wall with a loud boom which echoed and re-echoed.

'Oh, crumbs!' Emma put her hand to her mouth, not knowing whether to hide or attempt to escape.

Dr Shaw said, 'If she's in her third year she'll soon be on her way, and with luck you'll be your usual sunny self again.'

'Sunny self? My God!' Emma muttered, and with a sickly grimace mimicked Sister Darling as she said, oh so sweetly,

'Thank you, Nigel. You don't know what a relief it is to pour out my troubles to you.'

Emma thought she would throw up if she listened to any more of that tripe. Flinging open the door, she collided with a large, solid masculine figure, and looking apologetically into the face of its owner felt her bones lose their strength and a knotting in her stomach. He *must* know that she had overheard every word they said.

Dr Shaw steadied her with his hands on her arms and

looked down at her with a knowing, ironical smile in his hazel eyes.

'Ah, a new departure,' he said smoothly with the lift of an eyebrow. 'I wonder why I hadn't been told we were accommodating patients in the linen room. Is there anyone I should see?' He made a play of looking into the room over her shoulder.

She felt hot colour rush to her cheeks and had no idea what to reply. She knew what she would like to say, but that was out of the quesiton. He stared at her for a moment, then, as if he had completely lost interest in her, strode away.

She hurried across to the kitchen on wobbly legs. She hated him and she hated Sister Darling, and she was as anxious to get away from them as they were apparently eager for her to leave. Should she stay down in Cornwall, not bother to come back here? It was really tempting. But a fierce determination made her brown eyes turn even darker. If she *did* decide to do that it would be to please herself not to give them satisfaction.

Dr Shaw seemed very keen on Sister Darling, and Emma wondered why. Undoubtedly she was efficient, the doctors all kow-towed to her, and he would appreciate that. And when she wished, she could look attractive. As for him, he acted as if anybody below the rank of Ward Sister didn't exist and he was immensely pleased with himself. Imagine being married to either of them! That would be hell. But they probably deserved each other, and the best of luck to them.

It seemed a long morning, beset by Sister Darling watching Emma's every move like a vulture and appearing disappointed when she could find nothing to complain about. When lunchtime came Emma was delighted to see Nurse Keating was already in the canteen. Taking her scampi and salad, she went over to join her. She flopped on a chair and gave a loud sigh.

'Seeing you is sheer bliss, Debbie,' she said.

'Darling still on the warpath?' Debbie grinned.

'Need you ask! She created over us changing duties but finally agreed. Thanks again, love. Roll on the weekend!'

'You're very keen on Cornwall, aren't you? I'm surprised you ever left.'

'Now don't you start, I've had enough of that for one day. I overheard Darling telling Dr Shaw she wished I'd stay down there. Cheek!' Emma said indignantly.

Debbie split open her roll and buttered it. 'Are you glad you took up nursing?'

'Not when I'm working under Darling. I liked it on the other wards—most of the time. What about you?'

Debbie nodded cheerfully. 'Oh, I never wanted to do anything else. Never even considered it. All my aunts and my gran and mum were nurses and it seemed a matter of course that I should be one too.'

'Isn't that rather a bind, though, to be expected to keep up to their standards? I mean, there were two bad reasons why I took it up. One, because I didn't particularly fancy doing anything else and two, because I've got a cousin who's apparently, according to my mother, a second Florence Nightingale. She passed all her exams with flying colours and became Nurse of the Year. And I, silly idiot that I am, rather fancied myself following in her footsteps. What a hope! Now, of course, everything I do—or rather don't do—is compared with her. Can't win, can you?' Emma gave a rueful laugh.

'You aren't doing too badly, you'll pass your exams all right. What did you do in the year you were waiting to come here?'

Emma smiled reminiscently. 'I worked for the local vet. He's an awfully nice man, he said I had a way with animals. It was a bit smelly and noisy, but when you got a lick or a purr and knew someone's pet was getting better it gave you a lovely feeling of satisfaction.'

'Yet you never thought of staying on there? I mean, going in for it properly.

'Not really.' Emma frowned. 'I suppose I might have done, but I only went there after I'd been accepted here, and Mum and Dad were so chuffed at that they wouldn't have wanted me to chuck it. Come to think of it, I wouldn't have wanted to do that either. I was looking forward to coming here. What did you do?'

'Typing and shorthand, and I hated every minute. I liked my free evenings, though, there was a group of us, girls and fellers, and we had fun. Have you got a boyfriend?'

Emma considered that. There was Derek, but was he her boyfriend? He was good-looking and pleasant and they had usually gone to the Saturday night discos together. There was nothing you could dislike about him, but he was a dreamer, always building castles in the air, picturing the smart racing cars he was going to own—one day. He earned very little in a gents' outfitters, and was generous to a fault. Emma couldn't help wondering how he was ever going to save enough money to buy the expensive things he wanted.

'Ho, ho! Keeping it a secret, are we?' Debbie laughed.

With a start Emma came back to the present. 'No, I was just thinking. There is a chap I'm very fond of, but I don't think there's much future in it. How about you?'

Debbie shook her head. 'No, not at the moment. I'd hate to be committed to anyone yet, I want to play the field.'

'Looking out for a handsome doctor?' Emma teased.

'Handsome doctor!' sniffed Debbie. 'They're pretty thin on the ground and those you do meet wouldn't be seen dead speaking to a student nurse. Here, isn't it time you were getting back?'

Emma glanced at her watch and let out a squeal. 'I

don't believe it!' And without another word she rushed
from the canteen.

Friday evening arrived on leaden feet and with a
leaden sky to match. When it was time for Emma to
leave for Paddington and the night train to Penzance
some mischievous sprite pulled open the zip of the sky
and rain tumbled down like a waterfall. That meant
wearing an anorak, taking an umbrella and still having a
wet lower half in which to spend the night.

As she set off down the long puddled path to the
hospital gates, cars protecting their fortunate owners
passed her uncaring, the drivers anonymous behind
rain-blurred windows. As they waited the opportunity
to move out into the main stream of traffic on the busy
road which led to the town centre one driver leaned
across and wound down his window a little.

'Can I give you a lift?' he asked.

Emma turned to him gratefully and started to thank
him, when she recognised the hazel eyes and shook her
head. 'N-it's all right, thanks.'

He opened the door. 'Get in,' he ordered.

She backed away.

'Will you get in, please? You're holding up the
traffic.'

She did as he said, because he had that sort of
manner. But when she sat down she was thankful to be
out of the rain.

'Where do you want to go?' he asked as she fastened
her seat belt.

'To Paddington.' She looked at him apologetically.
'But I'm sure it's out of your way.'

'Not really. Anyhow, you're not dressed for this sort
of downpour.'

Emma rubbed her window futilely with her hand. She
wished Sister Darling could see her now. On the other
hand, if she did, the rest of Emma's time working with
her would be hell.

'What part of Paddington do you want?'

She glanced across at his perfect profile. This was the first time she had seen it at close quarters and at this angle. His hair was very fair and very straight, so how come he had such dark eyebrows and lashes? Did he dye those or bleach his hair? How was it that although everybody had two eyes and a nose and a mouth, some people were really plain, some just ordinary, and a few like Dr Shaw very handsome? It couldn't just be the way his features were set, so what the heck was it?

He glanced at her sharply. 'Where do you want me to drop you?' he repeated.

'Oh, I'm sorry. At the station, please, if that's not too much out of your way.'

'So you're off on your holidays?'

Was he pretending not to remember his talk with Sister Darling, or had he really forgotten because he didn't attach much importance to it?

'I'm going home to Cornwall for the weekend,' Emma said stiffly.

'Oh, so you are.'

Before she could stop herself she looked at him again and saw the corner of his mouth twitch. So he *did* remember and was laughing at her. The beast!

'I'm afraid I've made your car wet,' she said with relish as she saw that the rivulets of water had run from her umbrella.

He didn't even glance down. 'It will survive,' he replied casually. 'I've never been to Cornwall. Is it all it's cracked up to be?'

'It's beautiful, you really should go there.' Her eyes grew warm with enthusiasm. 'The scenery is out of this world, and there's St Michael's Mount! Mind you,' she added trying to be fair, 'inland it isn't so hot. If you just drive down there you only see the villages, but it's the coast and cliffs that are so lovely.'

'Wouldn't you like to work down there? The East

End of London can't possibly compete with it for beauty.'

A smothering sense of anger and disappointment swept through her. So he was hoping to help Sister Darling with her cause. How pleased he would be if he could say he had persuaded the 'dopey rustic' to return to her native land! In fiction she would probably have demanded to be put down out of the car immediately, but this was real life, and despite everything she was jolly glad to be out of the rain.

'I've signed on to do three years at Nightingale's,' she said coldly. 'Surely you don't suggest I should break my contract?'

They had stopped at traffic lights and he took the opportunity to look directly at her. Her heart for some unknown reason flipped up and down ridiculously as she saw the gold and green flecks in the irises of his eyes and his intent expression, as if he could see deep down inside her. No wonder Sister Darling had her claws set firmly on him. Who could blame her?

'I suggested nothing of the kind, Nurse,' he said mildly, 'I merely asked the question. But no matter.' He put his foot on the accelerator and they moved forward with the stream of traffic.

Of course he hadn't suggested she should leave, and she wouldn't have been so touchy if she hadn't overheard that conversation. Even if he hadn't guessed before that she had been listening he would know now because of her reaction. In future she would really have to remember not to listen to conversations not meant for her ears.

She was both glad and sorry when they reached the station. Glad because she felt awkward and embarrassed in Dr Shaw's company and was secretly sure that if he had seen who he was offering a lift to he wouldn't have stopped. But sorry because this once only trip with him was over. Though why that should bother

her she couldn't imagine.

He raised his hand. 'Glad to help,' he replied, looking in his rear-view mirror before easing out on to the main road.

Emma stood and watched his car, like a silver cigar, disappearing into the distance. She was early now, so she had time for some coffee and a sandwich. She took it to a plastic-topped table surrounded by luggage and people in wet raincoats and with dripping hair. She felt warm and cosseted, someone special. What would it be like to have somebody such as Nigel Shaw to be really keen on you, for his eyes to light up when he saw you and to greet you lovingly with a kiss? She shivered, not from the wet or the cold but because the picture she had evoked set her nerves tingling and her spine creeping.

Replacing her cup firmly on the table, she went out on to the platform. She was not going to indulge in those foolish thoughts. But later, despite the sounds and movement of the train, as she leaned back in her corner seat she drifted off to sleep, and green and gold-flecked hazel eyes and fair straight hair dominated her dreams.

CHAPTER TWO

EMMA WALKED stiffly from the train, stretched and breathed deeply the fresh salty sea air. Penzance was looking its best in this early morning hour with the sea sparkling in the sunlight, the brightly-sailed fishing smacks bobbing up and down in the harbour and over the sea wall St Michael's Mount, an avuncular monument, large and comforting, there to keep all danger at bay.

She walked slowly, stopping now and again to watch ships loading and unloading their cargoes. As she neared the pier-end muscular men with weatherbeaten faces hoisted up baskets of stiff iridescent fish and lobster pots of crayfish to be loaded on lorries for delivery to the morning auction at the Newlyn fish market.

Emma smiled at a young fisherman who had clambered up on to the quay.

'Could I buy a couple of these crabs?' she asked.

He looked from them to her. 'Fancy them for your breakfast?'

'I've just got off the train and I'd like to take them to my mum,' she explained.

His merry blue eyes considered her appreciatively. 'Didn't know it was Mother's Day.' He delved in the pot and took out two crabs and tested them for weight. 'There's a couple of good 'uns.' He laid them on the ground and they sidled slowly along. 'You'll need to watch our for their pincers, they'd give you a nasty nip. Got something to put them in?'

She shook her head.

15

'OK. Hang on and I'll get you something.'

He swung back on to the deck and after a moment returned with an old sack, strode across and popped the crabs in the bag, then felt in his pocket and brought out a piece of twine to tie it with.

'There you are. You want to 'ave a bit of salad with they.'

'Yes, I love crab salad.' Emma opened her handbag. 'What do I owe you?'

He grinned boldly. 'Give us a kiss, me darlin', that'll do fine.'

Without more ado he put his fishy-smelling arms around her and gave her a smacking kiss.

She laughed and pulled away. 'That's not fair, I didn't agree the price!'

He grinned mischievously. 'They ain't mine to give really, but never mind, don't suppose they'll miss 'em.'

Emma stared at him open-mouthed for a moment, but he swung down on to the boat and disappeared below deck.

After hesitating she hurried away, wishing she had decided to buy her mother some fruit or flowers, but the truth was she saw more than enough of those on the ward.

She leaned down on the railings of the promenade to look at the beach. It was not popular with visitors because it was shingle instead of sand, and children couldn't build castles. But when they were young she and Wendy, her sister, used to climb over the rocks and pick up winkles for tea. They were revolting, she thought now, with those horrid little plastic discs which you had to take out before you could eat the scrap of fish inside. She didn't think she could eat them now, they were nothing but sea snails—still, it was better not to think like that or you'd probably not eat anything. She was very aware of the movement in the sack, so she took a short cut home, wondering whether the family would be in bed when she arrived.

Houses nearby still had their front doors closed and the curtains drawn, but when Emma went indoors her mother came forward to kiss her.

She drew back. 'Ugh! Did you come on a fishing boat?'

'No, I bought a couple of crabs for you.'

Her mother looked taken aback. 'You never brought them down from London?'

Emma laughed. 'Not likely! I got them on the quay where they were unloading.'

'I wish you'd come home at a more reasonable time,' Wendy grumbled. 'I like to get up late on Saturdays, but I had to get up so that we'd all have breakfast together. As if it mattered!'

Emma sympathised. She couldn't imagine eating cornflakes in the company of your sister compensated for the loss of those hours in bed.

'Sorry, love, but that's the time the train gets in. Any complaints to British Rail.'

'Wendy is having her talk with the careers teacher next week,' their mother said later.

'Have you made up your mind what you want to do?' Emma asked her.

Wendy tossed her unruly auburn hair back. 'Yes, I want to be a model.'

'Don't talk nonsense,' her father scoffed. 'You and every other daft young girl! What you want to do is take up nursing the same as Emma, that's a proper career and one to be proud of.'

'Nursing? I'd hate it,' Wendy wailed, 'and if Emma told the truth I bet she hates it too.'

They turned to Emma in dismay. 'That isn't true, is it?'

At the anxious look on their faces and the worry in their eyes Emma knew that no matter how she was tempted to give up nursing she couldn't do it. She had to let them keep their dreams.

'Anyone would hate it unless they really wanted to do it,' she said. 'It's a lot of hard work and you have to be dedicated. There isn't much money in it either, but if you do like it there can't be anything more satisfying. How does hairdressing appeal to you, Wendy?'

'No, I want to be a model,' Wendy said obstinately. But Emma had seen a flicker of interest on her face when she mentioned hairdressing.

Their mother was eager to change the subject. 'I saw Derek in town yesterday, Emma, and he said he'd come for you at half past seven to take you to the disco. What a lovely boy he is! He always seems so pleased to see me, and he's very good-looking.'

He arrived on time, smiling as usual. His brown hair was neat and had a natural wave, and he looked smart in a brown striped suit and open-necked shirt. He greeted them all with friendly charm and handed Mrs Glover a bag of mushrooms.

'I picked them in the field behind our house,' he said.

'That *is* kind of you, Derek.'

She looked at him so fondly that Emma felt embarrassed. What with Sister Darling and Dr Shaw whispering sweet nothings to each other and her mother showing all that affection for Derek Emma wondered what it would be like to have someone feeling that way about you. And it just went to show how out of touch with reality she was when the face she momentarily pictured close to her own had green and gold-flecked hazel eyes gazing soulfully into hers. She gave a short derisive laugh which she turned into a cough when Derek turned to look questioningly at her.

'I'm looking forward to this. I wonder who'll be there?' she said.

It was good to see so many people she knew, girls and boys she had grown up with. It gave her a feeling of belonging which she never had in London. Her friends crowded around.

'Home again, Emma?'

'Gosh! You must be earning the earth, the times you pop down here.'

'I don't know how you can bear to leave London and all those theatres and shops.'

'D'you really like nursing?'

'Yuck! I'd hate it, all those sick people.'

'It's the uniform, isn't it?'

'She's going in for a proper career, but then she always had the edge on the rest of us.'

Mary Perkins, the least favourite of Emma's friends, who always looked at Derek with the same doting look on her face as Mrs Glover and stood very close to him whenever he asked her to dance, eyed Emma with a sour expression.

'I'm surprised you haven't found yourself a doctor by now, you usually get what you set out for,' she said.

Emma glanced involuntarily at Derek and felt sorry for him because the smile had left his face. She tucked her hand in his arm and led him on to the floor, clicking her fingers in time to the music, which saved her having to reply to Mary.

The next morning Derek walked to the station with her and bought some magazines from the stall.

'When will you be coming down again?' he asked.

She pulled a face. 'Not until my annual holiday, and the list hasn't been made out yet.'

'Your annual holiday? But that could be ages and ages. Why can't you come down at weekends again like you've been doing?'

Emma smiled ruefully. She knew that expense would mean little or nothing to Derek, who would spend first and wonder what to do for money afterwards.

'Because the half-price coupons have stopped now, I suppose it's because the summer is coming up.'

'Well, can't you manage it anyway? You're not as

hard up as all that, are you?' he frowned.

'I'm not exactly on the breadline, but the fares are pretty expensive and I need my money for other things. Living in London isn't cheap, you know.'

A dreamy look came into his eyes. 'All the same, it must be lovely. I'd hate to stay down here all my life—I want to travel, do exciting things. One of these days I will.'

Emma felt sad. Derek had so much going for him—looks, charm, generosity and ambition. But there was some quality missing and it was difficult to pinpoint it. She wished he might get the things he wanted, but doubted it.

The guard raised his flag and blew his whistle. Derek stepped away from the train and waved as it drew away.

Emma stood by the window and watched reluctantly as the view of the bay slipped away. Then she sighed and went to her corner seat. It was plain she would have to stay on in London and complete her training, and in her heart she had know all along that she must do that. It would not be for very much longer, though working under Sister Darling made every day seem endless. She wondered, not for the first time, just why the Sister seemed to dislike her so much and why that feeling was mutual. She had got on well enough on other wards. She thought back over that time, and gradually a possible solution dawned on her. As this was her final year as a student and it was leading up to her important qualifying examinations, she was perhaps not trying hard enough? Was Sister Darling really doing her best to make her more painstaking, confident and reliable? Emma felt a glow of self-satisfaction at coming to such a charitable conclusion and pulled a face, amused at discovering what a nice person she really was! The woman sitting in the opposite seat caught sight of her grimace and shrank bank into the corner with a scared look on her face. Emma was convulsed with laughter and took out her handkerchief to try and hide the fact, but not, apparently, with a great deal of success, for as they drew into the next station the woman gathered her things together and hastily left the compartment. Emma, looking out of the window, saw that the woman had not left the train and started to laugh again. This, she told herself sternly, must be an attack of hysteria. Pull yourself together!

Later on the truth of what she had thought struck her anew, for she didn't always behave like someone who would soon qualify to become a staff nurse. She mustn't be like Derek and dream about what she hoped might happen, she must do her utmost to bring it about. In future she would try and see that Sister Darling had nothing whatsoever to complain about.

When she got back to the hospital she discovered that although she had only been away for a couple of days changes had been made. After tomorrow she would no longer have a room in Residency but had been allocated one of three flatlets taken over by the hospital authorities in a house a bus ride away. She had always known that this might happen, for places in Residency were intended primarily for the use of newcomers, but having had a room there for so long she had expected to stay there until the end of her training. She looked at the list eagerly to see who the nurses in the other flatlets were, because that could make a great deal of difference. She saw that it was Nurse Bishop and Nurse Dark. Dorothy Bishop she knew slightly, she was a plump, fair-haired girl who could be amusing company but had the reputation of being a mischiefmaker. She'd have to watch out for that. Celia Dark? She searched her mind, but couldn't think who she was.

She started the week as she meant to go on, arriving on the ward punctual to the minute, her cap on straight, her dark hair brushed smoothly and carefully behind her ears with no wisps daring to escape. Her apron was arranged exactly and a pleasant, competent smile was

pinned on her face. She greeted each patient with
cheerful confidence, and when she assisted Nurse
Brown in making the beds she mitred the corners of the
sheets before tucking them in and plumped up the
pillows. She straightened lockers and removed anything
that was not strictly necessary, and replaced radio
headphones neatly on the hooks on the walls. These
were her usual duties, of course, but today she did them
swiftly and enthusiastically as if she had been on a
course of vitamin pills. And it made a difference.
Instead of feeling bored with the sameness she felt
pleased with her efforts and full of energy.

Sister Darling, making her ward round prior to the
arrival of Dr Shaw, looked round critically, eager,
Emma felt sure, for something to complain about, but
there was nothing, and Emma felt inordinately pleased.

Later, Nurse Brown asked Emma if she wanted to go
first for coffee. Emma glanced towards the ward doors
and glimpsed a white coat disappearing into Sister
Darling's room and said, for some inexplicable reason,

'It's OK, Betty, you can go first. I had rather a late
breakfast.'

This was not true, and Emma couldn't understand
herself. It must be this new feeling of vitality and
wanting to enjoy her work. She glanced again towards
the Sister's door and knew that today, at any rate, she
wouldn't be the topic of conversation and complaints.
Maybe this was why they came out fairly soon.

Emma saw the doors swing open and felt her heart
swing to and fro just as they did. The last time she had
seen Dr Shaw was when she had sat beside him in his
car, and she hugged to herself the knowledge that Sister
Darling knew nothing of that. She smiled at Dr Shaw as
he came towards her, but as he glanced her way there
was no answering smile on his face and she felt hurt,
although she knew quite well that student nurses were
always ignored by the doctors.

As Nurse Brown was not there she fell in behind them. Never before had she summoned up the courage to do that, and Sister Darling gave her a sharp, disapproving stare. Emma walked several steps behind them and stopped when they did at each patient's bedside. She listened, fascinated by Dr Shaw's voice and manner. Oh, he had the bedside technique all right. He was friendly and interested and questioned each patient and gave more information than was usual, she thought.

Mrs Crosbie, who was in for observation, was still in bed awaiting his arrival. He smiled and said he would take a look at her. Emma, without being asked, drew the curtains for privacy, and before Sister Darling could say, 'Sheets, Nurse,' she stretched across to turn them back. She gave a groan of despair as her eager arm cuaught the jug of orange juice on the locker and before anything could be done about it tipped its contents not only over Mrs Crosbie and her sheets but over Dr Shaw's jacket and in particular his sleeve. Emma froze. Dr Shaw swung around angrily and glared at her. Sister Darling said in a remarkably controlled voice,

'Fetch some towels, please, Nurse.'

Emma, too shocked to think straight, hurried to get them, but when she brought them back she couldn't think what to do with them. Sister Darling and Dr Shaw exchanged a look of resignation and Emma wondered what she had done wrong now.

'We'll need some damp tissues, please, Nurse—this stuff is sticky,' Sister Darling said as if talking to a young child.

Emma could have kicked herself. If she hadn't been so embarrassed by the accident she would have thought of that. Sister Darling was really being very sweet about it all. She hurried away and returned with a wad of damp tissues which she held out to Dr Shaw.

'I'm sorry, sir. Shall I help you off with your jacket?'

she asked.

He was still scowling as he said, 'I can manage.'

But Sister Darling helped him to remove it and murmured something which Emma didn't hear, but they flicked her a quick glance and smiled at each other. Just then his bleep sounded and he had to hurry away to answer the call.

'I'll be back to examine Mrs Crosbie,' he said as he left.

Sister Darling turned on Emma sharply. 'Is there no end to the damage you can do? Change those sheets immediately. And clear up the mess—and don't forget the floor. You can't expect the cleaners to deal with all your mistakes. And you'd better be quick about it. When Doctor returns I want everything to be ready for him, so get on with it!'

Emma should have realised that Sister Darling's gentle manner had been for Dr Shaw's benefit. She used the rest of the tissues to wipe the locker top and jug.

'I'm sorry about that, Mrs Crosbie, I'll just get a mop and do the floor and then I'll get you changed,' she said.

'I don't like that idea. I'm all sticky—you can't leave me like this!'

'I'm afraid I'll have to or this will be stepped all over the floor,' Emma explained. She fetched a bucket of water and a mop, and when that was done she took it away and fetched clean sheets and pillows.

'It's no good you doing that until I've changed my nightdress,' Mrs Crosbie whined. 'I haven't got another one until my sister comes, so what are you going to do about it?'

'I'll get you a hospital one,' said Emma, and fetched her the nicest one she could find, for she sympathised with the poor woman and understood her annoyance. But her sympathy tended to fade as Mrs Crosbie said as she helped her to change into it,

'You've blotted your copybook all right, Sister and

Doctor won't forget this in a hurry. Shame about his jacket, he's such a nice man too, but he looked really angry, and who can blame him?'

Emma ignored that and hastily made up her bed, this time with unmitred corners to the sheets.

'Are you usually so clumsy?' Mrs Crosbie went on. 'I've been in hospital many times, but I can't say anything like this has happened to me before. What are you going to do about my orange drink?'

Before Emma could reply she saw Sister Darling and Dr Shaw bearing down on her like two avenging angels. She thought she could see the eager glint in the Sister's eyes as she looked for something not yet done, but she was unlucky.

Dr Shaw glanced at Emma and said, 'Now perhaps we can get on.'

Emma began dutifully to turn back the sheet, but Sister Darling pushed her aside.

'I think we can manage, thank you, Nurse. I'm sure you can find plenty to do.'

Her words, so harmless, conveyed to Emma the unspoken message that they could manage better without her.

Nurse Brown was back, so Emma murmured to her that she would go for coffee. As she made her way to the canteen she paused for a moment at the main doors and looked out at the green lawns and the paths that led enticingly to the road which led to the station and freedom. Then she turned away with a sigh.

CHAPTER THREE

EMMA WAS off duty and about to go to her new flatlet. She looked around the room, opened the cupboard doors and drawers to make sure she was leaving nothing behind, then with a final, rather sad smile, picked up her suitcase and made her way to the bus stop.

This was a part of London she did not know. There was a street market busy with men and women doing their shopping, so she walked slowly, eyeing everything with interest. At a fish stall the fishmonger thrust his hand into a bucket of water and pulled out a slithering eel that writhed and wriggled as he chopped it up all the while inviting people to come and buy. The customer took the soggy newspaper parcel and stuffed it in her plastic bag, then turned to clip her young son around the ear as he tried to pocket a herring.

Stalls piled high with apples, oranges, grapes and tomatoes overhung by hands of bananas looked so tempting and inexpensive that Emma promised herself she would come here to do her shopping. There were stalls with crockery and glassware and cutlery and others with jumpers, skirts and jackets, and she would have liked to brouse around, but her suitcase was heavy, so she made her way through the jostling crown where shoppers carried long French loaves under their arms regardless of the sleeves that rubbed against them by passers-by.

A crowd of people waited for the bus, and when it arrived they pushed and shoved; quueing was apparently not done. Emma managed to get a seat and a large woman with two bags bulging with smelly overripe

fruit and vegetables plonked herself down beside her.
Every now and again Emma got a sharp dig as the
woman screwed around to scratch herself.

Many of the passengers appeared to be regulars, for
they shouted friendly but abusive greetings and there
was a great deal of talk and laughter. Emma wiped the
grubby window beside her with her hand and peered out
at the squalid houses where many windows were
boarded and at the side streets where children shrieked
and played, darting across the road with clever
avoidance of traffic, while dejected groups of men
stood on the corners.

Emma viewed the scene anxiously, for her flat must
be somewhere in this neighbourhood and she did not
relish the thought of returning here when she came off
late duty, when the stalls would have packed up and
left, the shoppers gone and only people spilling out
from the many small public houses left.

They arrived at the stop where Emma had to get off.
The fat woman took her time in allowing her to pass and
it was difficult to push her way to the doors, but at last
she was on the pavement.

Where now? she wondered. People of all nationalities
thronged the pavement and she doubted whether they
could help her. In the distance she saw a young woman
walking briskly towards her. She was wearing a short
black leather skirt and fun fur jacket.

Emma approached her with a smile. 'Could you tell
me where Court Street is, please?'

The woman's eyelashes were heavy with mascara and
her large mouth smeared liberally with lipstick, but
despite the make-up a thin white scar which ran from
her forehead to her ear was plainly visible.

She moved some chewing-gum from one side of her
mouth to the other. 'Yes, ducks, second turning on the
left.'

Emma continued on her way with a feeling of

depression. She felt certain the scar had been made with
a razor. Had it been done by a jealous husband or in a
gang fight? That sort of life was foreign to her, but she
had no doubt she would encounter it in Casualty, where
she must move before her finals.

Court Street was a slight improvement on the other
streets, the tall houses were Victorian and shabby with
peeling plaster and gates hanging drunkenly from
broken hinges. Number thirty-four was on a corner; it
had drab cotton curtains hanging at the windows. So
this was to be her home, and she was glad she would be
sharing it. She climbed the flight of steps which led to
the inexpertly painted front door, and told herself she
must beware of the broken step when she returned home
after dark. Inside was a small hall with closed doors and
a flight of linoleum-covered stairs which led to the first
floor. A radio blared, a baby cried and a man and
woman screamed abused at each other. When Emma
reached the landing she checked the numbers on the
doors and stood outside number six for a moment
before deciding to knock on the door, although she had
a key. She heard the door behind her open and turned to
see who was there. A middle-aged woman wearing a
stained stain blouse peered around the opening.

'Good evening,' Emma smiled.

The watching woman directed her long nose at her.
'No one's 'ome,' she said hoarsely.

'Aren't they? Thanks. Then I'll let myself in. I'm
coming to live here,' Emma explained.

'Oh yes?' The woman rubbed her nose with the back
of her hand and continued to stare as Emma searched
her bag for the key.

Only when she had let herself into the flat and closed
the door did she heard the other door close. She put
down her suitcase and looked around the sparsely
furnished room. There were three brown armchairs
which looked anything but comfortable, a wooden table

in the centre of the room and in a corner a small TV.
She tripped over the edge of the carpet when she walked
over to the window, where beige curtains hung
dispiritedly. She looked out on to a side road where
children kicked a ball while others rode their bikes
amongst them.

She turned back to view the room from this angle,
hoping it would show an improvement. On the
mantelpiece was a brass clock which had stopped at five
past eleven and flanking it were two unattractive
ornaments. An empty cigarette packet had been thrown
carelessly on the floor beside the overflowing
wastepaper basket. No, the room did not look better
from this angle. But it had the essential things, and she
could brighten it up with a few coloured cushions and
ornaments from the market.

The kitchenette was remarkably well equipped and in
the fridge were eggs and milk and cheese, while on a
shelf were tea and coffee bags. Emma opened a
cupboard and saw a fair supply of crockery and cutlery,
and in the adjoining one were cooking utensils.

A large room had been divided into three cubicles.
Emma felt like Goldilocks as she peeped into one and
then the othe before finding the one which was to be
hers. The bed looked like a hospital reject, but on the
mattress lay two sheets, two blankets, a bedspread and
two pillows. There was a cupboard, chest of drawers, a
mirror and a chair. If she bought a lamp with a pink
shade to stand on the locker beside the bed it should
look quite nice. She had to admit it was not luxurious,
but she was lucky to have a room to herself.

When she had made up the bed and unpacked her
suitcase she decided to have a bath. It was stained and
old-fashioned, but the water was hot and came out in
loud steamy bursts. Emma relaxed in the water and
began to feel clean again. The woman beside her in the
bus had made her feel itchy and uncomfortable.

She heard someone arrive, so she got out hastily and towelled herself, then put on her pyjamas before rubbing dry the ends of her long hair which had dangled in the water. She stood in front of the mirror and brushed it until the long nut-brown hair shone. Then she wiped out the bath, put on her housecoat and went into the living-room to see who had arrived.

Nurse Bishop sat in front of the one-bar electric fire, her plump legs spread wide, a cigarette dangling in her mouth.

'Hello, Dorothy, as you can see I've arrived. I felt so filthy I had a bath. Was that OK? I hope I haven't pinched all the hot water,' said Emma.

Dorothy Bishop surveyed her with smiling half-closed eyes. 'Not to worry, we've got an immersion heater. It's Emma, isn't it? So what do you think of the flat?'

Emma raised her shoulders. 'The flat is fine, it's clean and it's got the necessities of life, but I can't say I'm smitten with the neighbourhood. Actually I'm surprised the hosital put us here.'

'They didn't exactly put us here. When you're kicked out of Residency it's up to you to find somewhere to live. Some nurses found this flat and when they were leaving they told the SNO, and now it's on their list of suitable accommodation. How long were you in Residency?'

'Getting on for three years. I thought they'd let me stay until I left.'

Dorothy gave a yell of disbelief. Cigarette ash fell down her dress and on to the floor. 'Gosh! They turfed me out after six months—that's quite usual.'

'So I was lucky. But what about the other nurses who have to move out, where on earth do they go?'

'It isn't easy, because they have to be fairly close to the hospital and there isn't a lot of choice. Several of them are in this area and others are the other side of the market. The SNO advises us to live in threes whenever possible, she thinks there's safety in numbers,' Dorothy laughed ironically.

'I suppose there is. It isn't the flat that worries me, it's getting here when you come off late duty that I don't fancy. Have you had any trouble?'

Dorothy shook her head. 'Not really, and I've been here twelve months. Dear Celia, of course, thinks a rapist lurks on every corner.'

'Celia? Is that Nurse Dark? I don't think I know her,' Emma admitted.

'Pity you can't keep it that way. There's some tea in the pot if you want some.'

'Thanks.' Emma sat in the chair opposite Dorothy and cradled her cup in her hands.

'You were given the hints on safety, weren't you?'

Emma frowned. 'I don't think so. Who would have given them to me?'

'When you handed in your Residency key didn't they give it to you then?'

'Oh, that thing. I didn't read it, I shoved it in my bag,' Emma said guiltily.

'Then be it on your own head.'

'Why? What does it say?'

'The usual commonsense things. Don't go anywhere with anyone you don't know, etcetera.'

'Who would?'

Dorothy raised her thin eyebrows. 'That's what we all say. But Carol Harper—do you know her? She's on Gynae at the moment.'

'I think so. Small with ginger hair?'

'That's her, only she wouldn't thank you for describing her that way. She's auburn and petite. Right?'

'I'll remember that,' Emma laughed. 'So what about her?'

Dorothy crossed her legs and settled herself more comfortably before continuing. 'Well, she'd been to her dentist and had to walk back through the market. A well-dressed man came up to her—he could see she was a nurse, of course, by the way she was dressed. Well, he raised his hat and said 'Excuse me, but there's trouble in the market, fighting and whatnot. Would you care for me to escort you?'

'He sounds a right old-fashioned number! What did Carol say?'

'Well, she told us she had a good look around to make sure he didn't have a car lurking, then she said, 'Thanks very much,' and off they went.'

'Oh dear, I don't know what I would have done, do you?'

'I think I'd have told him to get lost. But he took her arm, and sure enough they came to this fighting, she said there was blood everywhere and she was jolly glad he was with her. When they got out he said he'd see her to the hospital.' Dorothy stubbed out her cigarette.

'That is where he and I would have parted company,' Emma said determinedly.

'Same here, but Carol said he was so pleasant and gentlemanly she didn't like to appear to distrust him.'

'Go on,' said Emma, eager to hear more.

'Well, he took her to the gates and then he said, 'You know, my dear, you shoudln't go anywhere with a stranger. As it happens I am respectable and harmless, but you weren't to know that. I advise you to be more careful.' Then he raised his hat and walked away.'

'Crumbs!' exclaimed Emma, 'What would she do another time? What would any of us do?'

If she had her time to go over again Emma decided she would not have come to London to do her training, it was such a vast, impersonal place with latent terrors that were things she had not had to contend with back home. She could have trained at Truro or Plymouth and *if* she passed her RGN she would have to move away to become a staff nurse, and then she would do her best to get taken on in the West Country.

She stretched out her feet to warm them by the fire. 'I think it's going to be nice here. We couldn't sit like this in the hostel, could we?'

'I'd much rather be at the hostel,' Dorothy said moodily.

'You would? Why?'

Dorothy took another cigarette from her handbag and made several attempts to light it. 'There's nothing to do here. I like going in the staff room and having a bit of a gossip. It's dead boring here if you're sharing with Celia, she's a pain in the neck.'

'Well, we're free to come and go as we like, couldn't we go to the flicks sometimes or to a disco or something?' Emma suggested.

'Not on my legs we won't—I think I've got varicose veins. I'm overweight, see?'

'Then a little exercise is the very thing.'

Dorothy held out a thick leg for Emma's inspection. 'I get enough exercise in the hospital.' She eyed Emma with narrowed eyes over a spiral of smoke. 'You're the prettiest student in your batch, aren't you?' she announced at last.

Emma stared at her incredulously. 'Me pretty? Don't be daft!'

'You are, you know you are. Your hair is a super colour. What rinse do you use?'

Emma lifted a tress of hair from her shoulder and examined it. 'I don't use one, it's only brown—dirty old brown,' she laughed.

'It's like one of those conkers,' said Dorothy.

'Oops! I hope I'm safe here with you, sweetheart,' joked Emma.

Dorothy ignored that. 'I used to think you used make-up on your cheeks. Do you?'

'Heaven's no! I've always hated their colour. I'd like to be pale and interesting.'

Emma was beginning to feel decidedly embarrassed, she had never expected Dorothy to say such complimentary things. She was nicer than she thought.

'I've never seen anyone with bigger, darker eyes,' Dorothy continued.

'Oh, stop fooling around,' Emma protested. 'What are you after?'

'Well who do *you* think is the prettiest student?' Dorothy persisted, her eyelids drooping.

Emma frowned and shook her head. 'I haven't thought about it.'

To her relief she heard the door being unlocked and Celia Dark came into the room, took off her raincoat and threw it on a chair.

'I'm bushed,' she said. Then realising that Dorothy was not on her own she turned to look at Emma. 'Hello, you're Emma Glover, aren't you?'

'That's right. Glad to meet you, Celia.'

She was a thin girl with fair frizzy hair and looked disgruntled. She lifted the lid of the teapot and grimaced. 'Cold and stewed, I suppose.'

'It hasn't been made all that long,' replied Emma, 'but I'll put on the kettle if you like.'

Celia poured a little and took a tentative sip. 'No, this'll do.'

After a while Dorothy said with relish, 'Emma says she can't think of any student who's prettier than she is. What do you think?'

Emma swung around indignantly. 'I didn't say that!'

'You did—those were your very words,' Dorothy retorted.

'But I——' Emma began.

Celia interrupted her. 'I don't think she's at all pretty. What's pretty about her? Red face, brown eyes and straight hair. I don't call that pretty.'

As Emma looked away in embarrassment she caught sight of a malicious glint in Dorothy's eyes.

'You rotten devil,' she said still preferring Dorothy to Celia.

Dorothy chuckled, but Celia looked as if she didn't like either of them.

The rest of the evening was dull, with wrangling over which TV programme they should watch. Emma went to bed early vowing that she must find someone who would be willing to explore London with her, but it would be difficult because off-duty times would have to synchronise, and the girls she knew and liked enough to go out with either had regular boyfriends or else lived in other areas, which made spur-of-the-moment outings impossible.

The bed was more comfortable than she had expected, and she slept well. She awoke to the sound of the baby crying, doors being slammed and the radio blaring again. She glanced at her watch, held it the other way round, then turned it back in disbelief. Surely it couldn't be that time! And—oh, heavens, she had that bus journey. She leapt out of bed, had a brisk wash, pulled on her uniform in record time, went into the kitchen where there was still some tea left in the pot, poured herself a cup, then dashed out of the flat.

As she turned the corner of Court Street she saw her bus leaving the stop and knew with an inner groan that she was going to be late. Her only hope was that she might slip into the ward when Sister Darling was not in her room. She began to think there must be a bus strike as she peered fruitlessly for the next one to arrive, and when it did she fought her way on, determined not to get left behind. In the morning light the area did not seem so down-at-hell or sinister, or else she had less time to dwell on it. She kept glancing at her watch and could scarcely wait for the doors to open before jumping off and running up the street.

Never had a path seemed so long or cluttered with slow-moving people as the one which led to the hospital entrance. Emma ran through the doors and to the lifts, pressed the button, waited impatiently, then pressed it again.

'Come on,' she urged, but it ignored her plea.

She ran for the stairs, up the two flights, and against all rules was running along the corridor when she collided with someone who was coming out of a room. Oh no! It was the same masculine figure that she had done this to before, only this time it was she who clutched at his arms to steady herself. Suppressing a shiver, she looked up into his hazel eyes, longing to stay where she was, holding him, but she knew she must hurry away. He released himself from her grip and stepped back a little. Fixing her with a cold penetrating stare, he said in a voice like a whip-lash,

'Why have you not pressed the alarm for the cardiac arrest team, Nurse?'

She shook her head. 'There's no c-cardiac arrest, sir?'

'Then which patient is haemorrhaging? Why haven't I been told?' His eyes were piercing.

She gave him a swift scared glance. 'N-nothing like that, sir.'

'Surely you haven't so disregarded the hospital rules as to run in the corridor for any other reason?'

Emma stared into his angry eyes as if she were a rabbit and he a snake. Then she dragged her eyes away to look desperately at the clock on the wall.

'I—I——' she stammered.

'You're late, Nurse.'

They both turned to see Sister Darling bearing down on them, straight-backed, her headdress stiffly starched.

'Yes, Sister. I'm sorry, Sister,' Emma said miserably.

Dr Shaw's hazel eyes travelled thoughtfully from one to the other of them.

'I'm afraid I detained Nurse Glover, Sister. You must blame me,' he said with a melting smile.

Sister Darling, glad to be rid of Emma, dismissed her with a nod. 'Very well. Get on with your work now, you're needed on the ward.

Dr Shaw opened the Sister's door and with his arm around her followed her into the room. Then the door closed and Emma heard them laughing with a degree of intimacy that caught at her throat like a noose.

She greeted Nurse Brown and attended to the patients as carefully as usual, but she felt crushed by a mixture of bewilderment, misery and gratitude. She had been dreading Sister Darling's anger, but it was Dr Shaw's she had to face. He had been so cold and angry and then for no reason at all had come to her rescue. Why? Could it ever be possible to understand a man like that?

Her heart knocked against her ribs as she saw him and Sister Darling come into the ward, and she hoped fervently that neither of them would reprimand her for anything, she felt unexpectedly vulnerable, as if she might burst into tears and she would rather die. To be on the safe side she went to the far end of the ward and quite unnecessarily took Miss Hooper's temperature again. She should have known that ploy would not work, when Sister Darling said loudly and sternly,

'Why are you taking the patient's temperature now, Nurse? That should have been done long ago.'

Emma could see Dr Shaw's face wobble and blur in front of her and she tensed, afraid to blink or even breathe in case any tears should fall. Then there was the most wonderful reprieve, for the doctor's bleep sounded, and with a brief nod to Sister Darling he hurried away and she returned to her room.

CHAPTER FOUR

EMMA, DOROTHY and Celia were sharing the pizza Emma had bought in the market on her way home. She was not yet accustomed to the daily journey to and from the hospital and often wished she still lived in at the hostel. It was difficult to know how to take Dorothy, but she knew only too well that Celia would be reserved and unfriendly, so sharing the small uncomfortable living room night after night was worse then being on duty.

'What do you know about this?'

Dorothy ate the last of the pizza, pushed her plate aside and leaning back in her chair surveyed Emma and Celia from half-closed eyes. They waited to hear more.

'One of my patients whose husband is some big brass in the theatre took a fancy to me, said I was the daugther she wished she had,' she said with glee.

Celia snorted derisively. 'She was hallucinating.'

'I hope she showed her affection by pressing a twenty-pound note in your hand,' Emma joked.

'Not quite.' Dorothy looked smug. 'But she did press two tickets for the musical show *Chess* in my eager palm.'

'Good lord!' Both girls stared at her wide-eyed.

'Would you like the other ticket?' Dorothy managed to look at the space between the two of them. Then just as Celia opened her mouth to reply she added loudly, 'Emma?'

Emma gave a swift glance at Celia and guessing her embarrassment said, 'What about Celia? Perhaps she'd like to go.'

39

'I asked you.' Dorothy fumbled in her handbag for a cigarette. 'There are plenty of girls I can ask if you don't want to come.'

'But I do—I'd love to,' Emma said hastily. Then, remembering Sister Darling she asked anxiously 'When are they for?'

'It's OK—they're for the Thursday matinee, and as you should be finished by two o'clock we should make it so long as we don't dilly-dally on the way.'

'That's great—thanks awfully.'

Emma felt sorry for Celia, but in all fairness she was not a person whose company you would seek. Either the show or the seats or both would not be to her liking, you could depend on that.

Over the next few days Emma disregarded Sister Darling's niggling complaints, brushing them aside as if they were flies at a picnic, annoying but something you must put up with. They paled into insignificance against the lovely treat ahead. She was afraid to mention the outing to anybody in case it should get to Sister Darling's ears, and then she would undoubtedly think of some good reason why she had to remain on duty.

'Two o'clock at the hospital gates prompt or I'll go without you,' Dorothy threatened at breakfast on Thursday morning.'

'Don't worry, I'll be there, unless Sister Darling locks me in the linen room. Even then I'd think of a way to get out.'

Emma was so excited she could not concentrate on anything. She even missed Dr Shaw's round because she went to coffee early hoping it would make the morning seem shorter. When she returned from the canteen Dorothy was waiting in the corridor.

'Where have you been? I've been hanging round here for ages—I'll get the sack!'

'No, they couldn't do without you,' Emma said with a smile. 'Anyway what did you want me for? I can't get away yet.'

'No, it's just to tell you I've given the other ticket to Sister Jennings——' Dorothy began.

'Pull the other one!' giggled Emma.

Dorothy raised her pencilled eyebrows. 'I'm not kidding. Sister happened to say how much she'd like to see *Chess* because she once met Tim Rice who wrote it, and the tickets were given me by a patient on her ward, so I thought it would be a good chance to get in her good books, which can't be bad.'

Emma gripped the ward door. 'But—but you'd already promised it to me,' she protested.

'Well, I knew you weren't all that keen.'

'Me? Not keen? Whatever makes you say that?' Emma stared at Dorothy wide-eyed.

'You know you weren't. When I offered it to you you asked Celia if she'd like to go.'

'That was only because——' She knew there was nothing she could say that would change the situation, so she turned aside.

Dorothy glanced up at the clock. 'Got to fly. I knew you wouldn't mind.' She scuttled away.

Nurse Brown looked disgruntled when Emma entered the ward. 'You've taken your time—I thought you'd scarpered. I'm dying for my break. Miss Holland's drip wants replacing. Mrs King is on two-hourly checks, starting now. The physio will be up any minute to attend to Valerie Sims and she needs to be taken to the toilet first. Right?' She hurried from the ward.

Emma was glad to be busy and so have no time to dwell on her disappointment, which had lodged like a weight in her stomach. When she went off duty she made her way to the canteen and bought a large lunch of ham salad, apple tart and custard followed by a cup of coffee in an attempt to console herself. She made the meal last as long as possible, for the afternoons stretched before her lonely and pointless.

The thought of returning to her dismal flat depressed her, so she wandered around the hospital grounds. Normally on an afternoon off she would have busied herself doing some washing, writing letters or shampooing her hair, but that would be such an anticlimax. A couple of doctors were playing tennis and she watched them for a few minutes, then went into the hospital and read all the notices on the boards in the corridors without having any idea what she had read. She walked through the Outpatients' Department which was crowded and noisy with the whining and crying of children. She stood and watched as ambulances returned and disgorged their patients. But she was not really watching; her body was there, but her mind was at the theatre seeing the crowds and hearing the music. She wandered off again beside the grass and the flowerbeds until she saw a bench outside the Medical Block and sat down. The sun was shining fitfully and the light wind was chilly, but Emma scarcely noticed. There were a thousand nurses in the hospital, and to think she had to share with Dorothy and Celia! She kicked aimlessly at a pebble that richocheted against a concrete pillar and hit the leg of a passer-by. He swung round and—oh, heavens—it was no unknown man, it was Dr Shaw!

He came purposely towards her. The stupid man, surely he was not going to complain? The stone could not possibly have hurt him—worse luck.

He towered in front of her. 'Do you want to catch a chill? Angling for some sick leave, hm?' One eyebrow was raised as he questioned her.

'I'm not cold or I wouldn't sit here,' she replied shortly.

To her dismay he sat down beside her. 'Is this your afternoon off?'

She nodded, knowing full well it was no way to behave to a doctor, but she didn't care.

'And you've nothing better to do than sit here?'

Emma stared disconsolately into space for a moment or two, then felt a desire to confide in someone. 'I was going to the theatre, but—but something turned up and I didn't get the ticket.'

She felt the burn of his eyes on her and glanced up involuntarily to see him looking so sympathetic that her heart filled with some grateful nameless emotion and she had to look away.

'How disappointing—I'm sorry.' He laid his finger briefly on her shoulder. After a moment or two he spoke again. 'Have you been home to Cornwall recently?'

So he remembered! 'No,' she said. 'The soap people have stopped doing the half-price coupons and there's no way I can afford the fare, just for a weekend. I'll have to wait until my annual holiday and go home then.' She had not thought she was feeling cold, but now she was very conscious of the comforting warmth of his large body beside her.

'I've got an idea,' he said, after a while. 'I have to go to Cornwall soon, perhaps I could give you a lift?'

Her heart leapt. 'Really? Do you mean it?'

'When do you next have a weekend off?'

'Next weekend,' she said, her brown eyes shining. Then they clouded. 'Unless——' She had been going tos ay, 'Unless Sister Darling finds some reason to cancel it,' but she remembered in time that she would be speaking of the woman he loved.

'Unless?'

She looked up at him and saw that his eyes were gently smiling, and for a brief moment it was as if they were sharing some pleasant thought. Then he rose to his feet.

'Let me know if you'll be free to come and we'll fix it up.' With a brief nod he left her.

Emma's mind was in a turmoil. Dr Shaw was not the

most friendly of people, but it didn't matter. He was
kind, so very kind. She determined that nothing and
nobody would stop her having that weekend off, even if
it meant losing her job. She gave a mirthless laugh. Of
course he might let her down as Dorothy had, and yet in
her heart she believed he would not behave like that but
would keep his word if it were humanly possible. Her
disappointment at missing the matinee suddenly seemed
of no importance, as she had the weekend to look
forward to. Even more than the pleasure of going home
was the knowledge that she would be spending all those
hours with Dr Shaw beside her, just the two of
them, and the thought for some inexplicable reason
made everything inside her seem fluid and
vibrant.

The afternoon was entirely different now. She spent a
pleasant hour or so in the market rummaging through
the odds and ends. She bought a yard of wide medicated
plaster at a fraction of the price she would have
expected to pay; a pair of sheepskin slippers for her
mother; some gardening gloves for her father and a fine
gilt chain for Wendy. She could not resist a multi-
coloured skirt with huge pockets for herself, and was
delighted with her purchases, they were all such
bargains. It was only later when she counted up the cost
that she realised ruefully that it might be wiser not to
visit the market often. But never mind, she was going
home and would have no fare to pay, not even half-
price.

On Friday at breakfast Emma told Dorothy she was
going home for the weekend.

'What time does your train leave?' asked Dorothy.

Emma hesitated, caution bidding her keep her plans
to herself, but unable to stop herself she said happily,
'I'm not going by train this time. I'm having a
lift.'

Dorothy's eyes became triangular with curiosity. 'I

don't call that a lift, it's a hell of a long way. Who are you going with?'

Emma's heart swelled with pride and pleasure. 'Dr Shaw is taking me there.'

After a momentary stare Dorothy's eyelids drooped to their usual place, half shielding her eyes. 'Oh, that accounts for it.' She gave a sly smile.

'Accounts for what?' Emma asked sharply.

Dorothy raised a shoulder laconically. 'Just something I overheard in the staff room.'

'What was that?' Emma had a feeling of apprehension.

'Oh—nothing.'

'It must have been something. Tell me what it was,' Emma persisted.

'Oh, just something Sister Darling said to Dr Shaw.'

'Tell me what it was,' Emma pleaded anxiously.

Dorothy raised her eyelids and looked hard at her. 'Sister Darling said, "And for God's sake leave her down there, Nigel." I wondered who they were talking about at the time.'

Emma swallowed what felt like a boulder. 'Wh—what did he say?'

'Oh, I went out the same door as I went in, so I didn't hear. But they both laughed.'

All Emma's pleasure melted like snow in strong sunshine. She would cancel the arrangement, see if she didn't. Just wait until Dr Shaw came into the ward, and she couldn't care less if Sister Darling heard her. What a horrible pair they were! But by the time she reached the hospital her spurt of anger had changed to a simmering rage. She was not going to let them spoil her weekend and disappoint both her and her mother. She would take advantage of his offer and just think of him as a taxi-driver whom someone else had paid. Thank heaven she knew where she stood.

Later that morning when Dr Shaw made his ward

round she left it to Nurse Brown to accompany him
and did not even glance in his direction as he was leaving
the ward, although she was aware of his every
move.

Promptly at two o'clock she waited beside his
Porsche in the parking space reserved for him. She had
a change of clothes at the hospital and had changed into
her new skirt and pink anorak. Her hair, freed from her
hat, cascaded down over her shoulders until it almost
reached her waist. Her cheeks were flushed and her eyes
darker than usual with a mixture of anger and
anticipation. As she waited she felt almost resigned to
the fact that some emergency might have occurred and
he would cry off. Then she saw him striding across the
lawn wearing beige slacks and a tweed jacket. His hair
shone in the pale sunlight and as he drew near she saw
that a green shirt echoed the green flecks in the iris of his
eyes. He gave her a melting smile, hypocrite that he was.
OK, if that was the way he was playing it then she could
be amiable too.

'Good girl, you're on time,' he said as he unlocked
the door. 'No difficulties about leaving?'

Emma would not have told him if there had been now
that she knew he and Sister Darling were in collusion.

'None at all,' she smiled.

'I suppose your family will be putting out the red
carpet for you?' he said when they were free of the
traffic.

'I hope they'll be pleased to see me—at least, my
sister may not be, because instead of getting a lie-in on
Saturday morning she'll be expected to get up so that we
have breakfast *en famille*. She objects very strongly to
that, and who can blame her?'

'She lives at home?'

'Yes, she's quite a bit younger than me and is still at
school. There was a boy who came between us, but he
died with he was a baby. Where is your home?' she

asked, realising she knew nothing of him.

'Oxfordshire. My father is a vet.'

'Oh, I spent a year working for a vet before I started at the hospital.'

'Did you enjoy it?'

Emma nodded enthusiastically. 'Very much. I sometimes wish I'd decided to take it up seriously. Cats and dogs are so sweet when they're ill, don't you think? They don't get old and wrinkled and crotchety. And when they're puppies and kittens they're adorable. I think they've got the edge on humans.'

Dr Shaw raised his eyebrows. 'A vet's work isn't chiefly with domestic animals, it's heavy going when cattle and sheep need attention. There *are* women vets, but I shouldn't have thought you'd have been very suitable.'

And you don't think I'm very suitable as a nurse, either, Emma thought resentfully.

'So what do you see me as?' she asked.

He glanced down at her and for a moment their eyes met.

'I'm not qualified to be a careers adviser,' he said. 'You'd probably make somebody an excellent wife and be a good mother.'

'Gosh, you're so old-fashioned! Hadn't you noticed that women can be just as good as men at practically anything?'

'Yes, I had noticed,' he replied.

They drove the next few miles in silence. The countryside looked beautiful in the red-streaked sky as the sun sank slowly in the west.

'Where will you be staying?' Emma asked after a while.

'At the Prince Albert Hotel in Penzance. Do you know it?'

'Yes, it's on the sea-front only a stone's throw from where I live.' She laughed reminiscently. 'When I was a little girl I used to think anybody who stayed there must be a millionaire, they looked so affluent—and stuffy!'

He looked amused. 'As I'm not particularly affluent I must be stuffy. At any rate, I have no doubt I would appear so to an immature person. We'd better get something to eat soon. Do you know anywhere decent?'

Emma searched her mind. 'I haven't done this journey by road for years, but I do remember stopping at the Jamaica Inn on Bodmin Moor.'

'Made famous by Daphne du Maurier. Have you read her books?'

'Some of them, especially *Rebecca* which I read several times. I did enjoy it very much.'

'I seldom read fiction, but I saw *Rebecca* as a film and that was good.'

Emma turned to stare at him. 'You don't read fiction? You don't know what you're missing. So what hobbies have you got?'

'I like golf and when I see a beach I look out for quartz which I later have polished. I have some very lovely pieces from various parts of the world.'

'Then Cornwall is just the place for you,' Emma said enthusiastically. 'On the beaches you can sometimes find amethyst and rose quartz, and at The Lizard the rocks are made from serpentine. There are lots of small workshops on the cliffs where you can see it being polished and made into ornaments for tourists. I think you'd enjoy seeing that.'

'I'm sure I would, but I won't have time on this trip. Maybe I will at a later date. Thanks for telling me.'

They came to a crossroads where a long low white building decorated with fairy lights was situated on a corner.

'This looks promising, what do you think? Shall we

give it a whirl, or would you rather press on?'

'Let's try this—I'm hungry.' Emma was about to open her door when he said,

'Would you mind awfully not addressing me as 'Doctor'? Perhaps you'd call me Nigel?'

'Oh—yes, all right,' she replied, tensing her stomach muscles. Gosh, fancy calling him Nigel!

'And if I call you "Nurse" people will surely think I'm in my second childhood. I don't think I know your name?'

'It's Emma. Not very pretty, but I'm stuck with it,' she grinned.

It was a pleasant, busy bar with a dining area set apart. Nigel had a few words with the barman, then turned to Emma.

'What would you like to drink while we're waiting for a table?'

'A sweet sherry, please. I see there are a couple of seats over there, shall I grab them?'

There was a warm friendly atmosphere and around the bar much talk of the prices fetched by horses at the sale that afternoon.

'That reminds me of home,' said Nigel. 'My father was very involved with horse sales.'

'Didn't that make you think of becoming a vet yourself?' asked Emma.

'Yes, when I was very young. But later, laziness took over, and when I heard him going out at night while I was cosily in bed, and knew he would probably be tending animals in difficult labour, I confess I changed my mind.' he said with a wry smile.

'What about doctors? They can be called out at night too,' Emma reminded him.

'If you're on call, but with Father it could happen night after night if he was unlucky. It's very tough work and you have to have a way with animals—that's essential. I don't think I've got that.'

A pretty young waitress brought them massive menus. Emma studied hers, her mouth watering in anticipation. Nigel decided on grilled trout with fresh vegetables, but Emma knew that she could buy fish in the market and cook it easily. She wanted something different. There was duck in lemon sauce or chicken casserole, both of which she might have at home. But fillet steak was something she could never afford to buy, so she chose that with mushrooms, tomatoes, sweet corn, peas, cauliflower and new potatoes. Only when she had placed the order did she wonder about paying for it. She would surely have to, there was no reason why Nigel should. She knew she had nothing like enough money in her purse. Would it be all right to give him an IOU? If only she hadn't been so greedy but had settled for something simpler like an omelette, which however she didn't much care for. She shot him an occasional anxious glance. Should she pretend to be too ill to eat?

Still worrying, and very silent, Emma did as she was told and went to the table indicated. Then the food was brought, and it looked so delicious that she pushed her qualms to one side. When some people couldn't pay a bill they did the dish-washing. She could offer to do that, but it would be embarrassing. But that was in the future, and now she enjoyed every mouthful and throwing caution to the winds ordered a raspberry meringue with ice-cream afterwards, although Nigel had cheese and biscuits.

When they were drinking their coffee Emma knew it was a meal she would never forget, like a dream come true, with Nigel there beside her. Then the bill was brought, and she began to think her dream would turn into a nightmare. She watched him as he checked the items, then she ran her tongue across her dry lips and in a voice that shamed her by coming out in a squeak, said,

'Do let me know what my share is.' At which her

heart started to thump.

It seemed a lifetime before he slowly raised his eyes and smiled.

'No, Emma, it's been a pleasure to have your company.'

She felt unbelievable relief and was delighted that he'd said he was pleased to have her company, although no doubt it was said out of politeness.

When they left the inn she glanced up at the clear sky. 'Oh, look! A new moon. Say the name of a poet and a town and then wish. You mustn't say anything else,' she told him, her eyes shining.

'Tennyson. Cambridge.' He was silent for a moment, then he turned to her. 'Right, I've wished. Promise me it will come true.'

She laughed. 'These superstitions don't come with guarantees. You might have wished for a million pounds and I can tell you you'd be unlucky.'

'Aren't you going to wish?'

'It's no good, because I spoke first, and you mustn't do that.'

When they were driving away he said, 'I suppose, being Cornish, you believe in all that nonsense?'

'Now you *have* blown your chances! You don't call magic nonsense or else——'

'Then I quiver in my shoes. Tell me about some Cornish superstitions.'

'That new moon lark isn't necessarily Cornish, but we have plenty of our own. There's a stream near my home and my friends and I used to stand on the little wooden bridge and wish as we threw a leaf in, then we'd rush to the other side and if it was sailing through then that wish would come true. Sometimes they'd get caught up on a twig or stone and we'd swear that it wasn't our leaf that had done that. There was a lot of cheating, as you can imagine.'

'I wonder what a child has to wish for.'

'Toys, treats, possibly boyfriends when they were slightly older.'

'And you? What did you wish for?'

Emma laughed. 'I'm not telling!'

'Tell me some more.'

'Let me see. There are any number of stories of giants and ghosts, and legends about mines in particular. It's a fascinating county if you're interested in that sort of thing. There are old Roman remains, especially at Chysauster. But you want magic. Oh, I know—there's the Wishing Well at Madron, now that's really legendary and once upon a time was reputed to have curative powers to rival Lourdes—I don't know what proof there is of that. Anyhow, you have to have a pin to wish there.'

'A pin?'

'Yes, you throw it over your shoulder as you make the wish.'

'Right. I'll make sure to be properly equipped when I go there,' Nigel promised.

It was a lovely night, mild and clear, and as they drove along the tree-lined secondary roads Emma had never imagined such bliss. To be with Dr Shaw, who had seemed someone so apart, so untouchable, and to be calling him Nigel, and wining and dining with him, was unbelievable. Lucky Sister Darling, to know that he was hers. She wondered what Nigel liked about her. She must be completely different when she was alone with him. Emma stole glances at him just to reassure herself that he was there beside her and was as attractive as she remembered.

'They're building a splendid new hospital in Cornwall, between Lelant and St Ives. Did you know?' he asked after a while.

'No, I didn't know. What's going to be so splendid about it?'

'It will have all the latest equipment, excellent

theatres and a medical research centre. They'll be advertising for staff shortly. Would you care to have a look at it?'

Hurt and disappointment swept through Emma like a flame. He had sounded casual enough and normally she would have seen no harm in what he said, but after what Dorothy had overheard she realised his aim was to get her to apply to go there and he could return to his lady-love and tell her he had gone some way in accomplishing her mission. He was a two-faced beast, but she was a step ahead of him.

Pretending to stifle a yawn, she said, 'Thanks, but no, thanks. I've seen enough of hospitals and I want to keep clear of them over the weekend. Anyhow, one hospital looks much like another.'

He made no reply. Sulking, I suppose, Emma thought gleefully. But the glee was on the surface, beneath it she felt bereft. It had all been so lovely until now.

Later Nigel pointed out a large new building on the horizon. 'There it is, the new hospital. I'm thinking of applying to go there, but naturally I want to look it over first.'

She felt a rush of dismay. Why, oh, why was she so touchy, so eager to think badly of him?

'Then do let's go there,' she said.

He shook his head. 'I shan't be going there tonight. And of course you won't want to spend any of your precious time there—it was thoughtless of me to suggest it.'

So she'd blown it. She could have spent part of yet another day with him, they could have discussed the hospital together, and now she had thrown that opportunity away. It served her right.

'So you would like to work in Cornwall,' she said unnecessarily.

'That's why I've come down here—to see for myself the conditions and what the neighbourhood is like.'

Then, all too soon, they were driving across Penzance promenade and Emma pointed out his hotel to him. 'And I live first right and then right again.'

He stopped the car outside her tall terraced house and leaning across her opened the car door.

'Thank you so much for bringing me down here and for—for everything. It's been lovely. When will we be leaving to go back?'

'On Sunday afternoon. I'll call for you at two o'clock, if that's all right?'

'Thank you.' She stepped reluctantly from the car.

'I was wondering if you'll be free tomorrow afternoon?'

'Why, yes.' She knew she would be free whenever he liked.

'Then would you show me around some of the beauty spots? In particular the Wishing Well. I could do with a few wishes coming true.'

'Yes, I'd like that. Don't forget your pin,' she laughed, feeling happier than she had thought possible.

'Good, then I'll call around two—I can't say exactly.'

'I'll be waiting,' Emma smiled, and watched as he drove away.

CHAPTER FIVE

SLEEP ELUDED Emma, her mind was filled with the excitement of the day and thoughts of tomorrow. Where should she take Nigel—not to Madron first, in case he then thanked her and brought her home. No, she would leave that until last. They could start off by going to Mousehole, look at the many small shops on the quayside, then go on to Lamorna where many artists had studios and painted the wonderful cliff scenery. There was a small café there where they might have tea—or should she bring him home for that? But if she mentioned it to her mother she would be sure to go to no end of trouble and if Nigel didn't stay there would be disappointment all around. It would be better not to do that. After Lamora they could go to St Just and Carn Gloose, a beautiful stretch of moorland overlooking the sea. From there they could take the Zennor road, and she would tell Nigel the legend of the mermaid and if he wished they could drive to the church in the village where a carving of the mermaid was on the pew end and then take the Zennor road to the Wishing Well. Whatever they did it was going to be a wonderful weekend if the weather held. At last she slept, a happy smile on her face.

When she awoke it was indeed a fine day, and her mother suggested they went into the town together.

'So long as we're back in time for lunch,' said Emma. 'Dr Shaw is calling for me at two o'clock.'

'My, he's being very attentive, isn't he?' her mother said, looking smugly pleased.

'It's only because he wants to see the neighbourhood and knows I can show him the places he should see,' Emma replied, wishing that were not the truth.

'Would you like to bring him back to tea? I think that would be nice. I can get some splits and cream and I've got plenty of my home-made cakes,' Mrs Glover said.

'I'll see how things turn out, but don't put yourself out, because he may have made other plans.'

The shops, so different from those in the East End, had nevertheless a charm of their own. Some sold sheepskins and handmade sweaters and cardigans, and in the baker's there were bright yellow saffron cakes dotted with currants, wedges of thick heavy cake and Cornish pasties. In the Cornish stone shop windows were great slabs of rock split open to reveal purple, pink or white quartz. Nigel would be interested in those. If only there were more time she could show him so much. Perhaps they could return from Madron through the town, but there was the difficulty of parking.

'This Dr Shaw,' her mother said as they sat in a café in the town having coffee, 'Is he serious about you, do you think?'

Emma felt everything inside her curl up, shrivel and die. Under no circumstances would she bring Nigel back to tea.

'Heaven's no!' she said vehemently. 'He—he doesn't even speak to me in the hospital unless it's to tell me off. He's going to marry the Ward Sister—he only came down here to look over a new hospital that's soon to be opened near Lelant, and he offered me a lift because he knew I lived here.'

'Getting married, is he? That's a pity. I know Derek's a lovely boy, but I reckon you could do better. It would be nice to have a doctor in the family.'

Emma stifled a groan. 'Doctors aren't all they're

cracked up to be, and they don't even know that student
nurses exist. For heaven's sake—if he knew you were
thinking his bringing me down here meant anything
he'd leave me to make my own way home, and that's a
fact.'

'Oh well, perhaps when you're a Sister it will be
different.'

'When I'm a Sister? That's a lifetime away. I'll
consider myself lucky if I ever make staff nurse.
Anyhow, if I do, after a few years I think I'll withdraw
what there is of my pension and with my savings go
abroad for three months, preferably to America. I don't
want to feel I'm stuck in a hospital for the rest of my life
without seeing anything of the world.'

Mrs Glover clicked her tongue. 'I hope you won't do
anything silly. You need all the hospital experience you
can get, without breaking it, if you want to get on like
your cousin.'

'It's all in the future, I don't want to even think about
it yet.' Indeed, all Emma wanted to think about was the
afternoon ahead.

Dinner was chicken salad, and as soon as it was over
Emma went upstairs to get ready. Most of her clothes
she kept here, so she chose a green trouser suit which
would be sensible if they had to climb over rocks; she
brushed her hair which was still damp from her shower
and tied it back with the green ribbon knotted carelessly
as she had seen in a magazine picture, with one end
dangling. She sat in front of the mirror to put a smear of
eye-shadow on her lids. If only I had green flecks in my
eyes they'd match my suit, she reflected, seeming to see
Nigel's face beside her own.

It was almost two o'clock when she heard the car
arrive and bounded down the stairs to open the door
before her mother could reach it and maybe invite Nigel
in and trot out some embarrassing remarks. She opened
the door cautiously and stared at the caller in dismay—

for it was Derek who stood there. A Derek dressed
differently from anything she had seen him wear before,
a cap which didn't really suit him, a long red and black
striped scarf wound twice around his neck and a red
sweater with black and white motifs. She was about to
ask if he was going to a fancy dress party when
something made her stop.

'Well, hello,' she said, ready to laugh with him when
he told her the joke.

He had a broad grin on his pleasant face. 'Wendy told
me you were coming home. I'm so glad, because I've
got something to show you.' He took her arm and led
her outside to where a red TR7 stood beside the
kerb.

'What do you think of that?' he asked excitedly.

'It's super! Whose is it?'

He could scarcely speak, the words tumbled over each
other. 'It's mine, Emma, my own sports car—what I've
always wanted. And it's red! I've just taken delivery of
it, and—and——'

At that moment a sleek silver grey Porsche drew up
beside it and Nigel stepped out, dressed casually but
smartly in beige slacks and sports jacket.

Emma's heart had a fight on. It wanted to leap with
pride and joy as she saw Nigel, but it also sank because
it didn't want anything to dim Derek's pleasure.

'Hello, Nigel,' she smiled, trying to hide her
mixed feelings. 'Meet Derek Barnes, a friend of mine,
who's just bought his first sports car. Isn't it
lovely?'

Derek had been eyeing the Porsche with envious
admiration. When he looked up there was a cloud in his
eyes, and Emma could have wept.

'Derek, this is Dr Shaw who works at my hospital and
very kindly gave me a lift here.'

The men shook hands, then Nigel walked around the
TR7, and said, 'May I?' indicating the bonnet. He eyed

the engine and nodded appreciatively. 'It's good,' he said.

'Do you think so?' Derek looked up at him trustingly. 'Mind you, I haven't paid for it, it's on the never-never, but if I waited until I could afford to buy it outright I'd never get it.' His smile broadened. 'I've only just picked it up, and I came round right away because I wanted Emma to be the first one to ride in it.' He opened the car door and looked at her with wistful anxiety.

Emma's heart sank. She looked at Nigel. 'But I——' she began.

Nigel gave an almost imperceptible shake of his head and a slight silencing gesture with his hand.

'Then off you go and enjoy yourselves.'

Emma had no intention of being deprived of her outing with Nigel. 'Oh, but——'

Nigel gave her a fleeting frown. 'You want to tell your mother?' he said.

She turned and went indoors. She knew that Nigel wouldn't take her out now, so she had to make the best of things. Of course she didn't want to disappoint Derek, but oh, she did want to spend the afternoon with Nigel! Pinning a smile on her face, she returned to the waiting men.

'I've brought my cardigan in case it's cold,' she said, climbing into the TR7.

As Derek was going around the car she murmured to Nigel, 'When shall I see you?'

'I'll be in touch.' Turning to Derek, he sketched a salute. 'Now drive carefully, old man, you've got a mean machine there.'

Derek grinned selfconsciously, then started the engine, pressed the accelerator, and they shot forward. Emma, looking back over her shoulder, saw Nigel get in his Porsche, reverse, then drive smoothly away, and she ached with a feeling of tremendous loss.

'Where shall we go?' Derek asked, his eyes shining.

Emma knew she couldn't dampen his pleasure. 'I don't really mind, but let's drive around, because I'm sure you don't want to park it somewhere. I want to see how it goes.'

'I'm glad you feel like that too. It's a beauty, isn't it? It's T registration, but it's in good nick.'

'I can see that, it looks brand new.'

'Do you think so?' he asked happily. 'What I really want, though, is to have a Porsche like that doctor chap. And in silver grey. Then I'll feel I've arrived.'

'Oh, Derek, you'll never be satisfied. When you've got a Porsche what then?' she asked fondly.

He laughed. 'A Ferrari, I suppose. But most of all I want to go to America. Not for good, but just to see what it's like over there. I don't want to stay down here all my life.'

'That's a coincidence. I was saying the same thing to Mum only this morning.'

'Life is so exciting, isn't it? You never know what will happen next. Who would have thought just a year ago that I'd own a car like this?'

Emma felt a flood of maternal affection, and she appreciated what Nigel had done. He had cottoned on so quickly, stopping her from saying that she had arranged to go out with him. Not many men would have done that. An unhappy thought wormed its way into her mind. Cancelling the outing probably meant nothing to him, he could drive around and see many beautiful places without her being with him.

'Shall we drive to St Ives and call on my Auntie Gladys? I'd love her to see my car.'

Emma's heart sank. They would be sure to stay there to tea, which would mean that if Nigel called for her in the evening she would miss that too.

'That's an idea,' she said brightly.

As she had guessed, they spent hours with his aunt,

a chatty lady, and it was late when they reached home.

'Thanks for taking me out in your lovely car, it's a beauty. This is cheerio now, because I'll be leaving to go back tomorrow.'

'Oh, I was hoping to see you in the morning.'

'Sorry, I won't be able to manage that—you know, things to see to.' Surely Nigel would arrange that they should meet in the morning and maybe go to Madron. She was not going to risk missing an outing with him again.

When she got indoors her mother nodded towards the mantelpiece.

'There's a letter for you there.'

'A letter?'

'A good-looking fellow called and asked if you were in. When I said "no" he handed me that. I think it must have been the doctor.'

She went on talking about him and his appearance, but Emma was thrilled to hold his letter. Murmuring, 'Must go to the loo,' she ran up to her bedroom.

She held the crisp envelope in her hands for a moment as a feeling of warmth and excitement swept through her. Then carefully she opened the envelope and took out the sheet of hotel-embossed paper.

Her eyes blurred for a moment. Then she read in his somewhat illegible handwriting,

Dear Emma, I have an appointment to see over the new hospital tomorrow afternoon so will be unable to drive you back. Be sure not to miss your train, you'd better check the time. Your ticket is enclosed. Yours, Nigel.

Disappointment so gripped her that she felt herself shaking. Rolling the letter into a ball she threw it across the room. Then her tears fell, hot scalding tears which did nothing to alleviate her unhappiness. Flinging herself on her bed, she buried her face in the pillow, which soaked up her tears. After a while she sat up and asked herself why she was crying. She had had her weekend home, a pleasant trip down and a ticket for her return. She ought to be laughing. She couldn't be crying because she had missed out on being with Nigel, could she? If so she was completely out of her mind, for he belonged to Sister Darling and even if he didn't he would have no interest in her. She took a paper tissue from her pocket and dried her eyes, then picked up the crumpled letter and smoothed it out. Returning it to the envelope, she put it in her drawer.

In the morning when she awoke it was raining, and she was glad, for even if she hadn't been leaving on the train it was not a day to go sightseeing. Her father drove her to the station across the wet, deserted promenade, past the Prince Albert Hotel. Emma turned to look at the windows, hoping that she might perhaps glimpse Nigel, but there was no sign of life except in the glass-covered porch where some guests were reading the Sunday newspapers. In the harbour the boats stood motionless, the men no doubt below deck drinking tea and playing cards. The warehouses looked shabby and empty and only an occasional cyclist passed them on the road.

'There's no need for me to wait to see the train out, is there?' her father asked.

'No, Dad, you get back. I think there's snooker on the box.'

'Yes, there is. OK then—cheerio.' He almost missed her cheek as he bent to kiss her, and she saw him drive on and towards the town to save having to reverse.

The platform looked deserted and dismal with no air of excitement as the plastic-hooded passengers boarded the train. Emma found a corner seat with no difficulty and tried not to think of the car journey she was missing. For once Penzance held no appeal. Instead of remembering the happy times she'd had when she lived here she recalled more clearly the days when things had gone wrong at school and when the holidays had seemed unending, with nowhere to go and nothing to do. When she was in London she tended to think only of the good times. It was as well to remember that wherever you were it was never a hundred per cent good or bad. She wondered whether Nigel would find what he was seeking at this new hospital and if he would move down there. And if he did would Sister Darling join him? It would be an ironic twist of fate if instead of them getting rid of her down here she got rid of them. As for herself—where would she go, what would she do?

But she was jumping the gun. First of all she must pass her examinations so that she would become a staff nurse. If she failed them it would mean another year at Nightingale's and very probably under Sister Darling, a fate she would not wish on anyone. But it could surely happen unless she spent more time studying. For the next few months she must concentrate on that.

She dreaded the sneering questions Dorothy would be sure to ask on her return, but she must face them. Celia would probably be out at some church meeting. But when she reached her flat she was relieved to find it was empty. She showered and changed into her night clothes, made herself an egg on toast and coffee and went early to bed. She took with her textbooks and notebooks, intending to make a start with her studying, but she was unable to concentrate. Instead she found herself thinking of Derek and his sports car and Nigel with his quick understanding, and they way she had messed things up by saying she had no interest in the new hospital. She heard Dorothy and then Celia return, the murmur of their voices, and then she slept.

CHAPTER SIX

'AND WHERE were you when I got back last night?'
Emma asked at breakfast.

Dorothy looked less smug than usual and there was
an expression of resignation in her eyes.

'Heather and I signed on at an agency, so I was
working at St Peter's yesterday.'

'But that was supposed to be your day off,' Emma
said in dismay.

Dorothy yawned. 'I know. I don't know how long I'll
be able to keep it up, but the pay is good.'

Emma knew she herself never had money to spare,
but she had no need to do agency work.

'Are you all that hard up, then?'

'No, I can manage, but Heather—that's Nurse
Wills—and I want to go somewhere abroad for our
holiday and we need money for that.'

'But you'll be too whacked to enjoy it if you get
overtired. Where do you want to go?'

'We haven't decided, but I'd like somewhere hot and
sunny so that we can just laze. I couldn't possibly go
sightseeing, it'd be far too tiring.'

'It'd certainly be something to look forward to and it
sounds great. I'm quite envious.'

'How did your weekend go?' asked Dorothy, but
without her usual curiosity.

Emma realised that with luck she would not have to
endure cross-questioning. Glancing at her watch, she
said,

'Heaven's, I always forget I've got that wretched bus
to catch—I must fly. The weekend? Oh, great!

Cheerio.'

Emma joined the crowd of people who trooped through Outpatients. As she passed the reception desk the SNO's secretary caught sight of her.

'Oh, Nurse Glover, I was about to leave a message for you. Miss Gow wants to see you at ten-thirty in her office. OK?'

'Righto, thanks,' Emma said weakly.

Now what had she done wrong, was it perhaps a crime to accept a lift from a doctor? If so then that piece of information would have been passed to the SNO by Sister Darling. With a sinking heart she wondered if there was some job she could do other than nursing where she was constantly made to feel totally inadequate.

The ward round was made by Dr Fellowes, so Nigel was not back yet, and Emma prayed that he hadn't met with an accident. He probably hadn't, because Sister Darling seemed in a better mood than usual. In fact she was quite skittish with Dr Fellowes and fluttered her eyelashes at him and skipped across the ward to join him after being called away. It made Emma wonder whether perhaps she and Nigel were not so committed to each other as she had thought. Emma deliberately allowed her thoughts to wander in this way to keep her mind off her forthcoming interview, but the clock moved inexorably on until she was forced to knock on Sister Darling's door to ask permission to leave the ward.

'Oh, it's you—and what do you want?'

'I have an appointment with the SNO at ten-thirty, Sister, so may I go now, please?'

'Of course you may. If she's asked to see you that's an order. You'd better hurry—and hurry back too. I don't want you to make this an excuse for an extra long coffee break.'

'No, Sister. Thank you, Sister,' Emma said humbly

as she had done a thousand times before.

She barely knew Miss Gow, but she could hardly be more unpleasant than Sister Darling, so she made her way to her office in a resigned frame of mind.

Miss Gow, grey-haired and bespectacled, looked up when Emma entered. She seemed tired as if she would welcome early retirement. She gazed at Emma for a moment as if wondering why she was there.

'You wished to see me. I'm Nurse Glover,' Emma reminded her.

'Ah yes.' Miss Gow selected some papers from a pile on her desk and scanned it briefly. 'Nurse Glover, I see you're nearing the end of your three years' training and your exams will soon be coming up. How do you feel about them?'

Emma gave a wry smile. 'Apprehensive, Miss Gow. But I'll do my best.'

'Yes. According to your report you don't seem to be making as much progress as we would hope.'

Emma might have known. That would be Sister Darling's report on her.

'I'm sorry about that, Miss Gow. Might I know in which way I've failed to give satisfaction, please?'

Miss Gow read the report again. 'There don't seem to be any specific reasons. Let me see—"She does not instil confidence in her superiors that she is competent to carry out her duties without supervision",' she quoted. She glanced up at Emma. 'It's essential to have that quality, you know. Are you lacking in self-confidence?'

'I haven't always been, Miss Gow.'

The SNO looked back over previous reports. 'I notice there've been no such complaints about you before.' She was silent for a moment, then she asked almost casually, 'How do you get on with Sister Darling?'

Emma hardly knew what to say, so she remained

silent, it being, reputedly, golden.

Mis Gow took off her glasses, rubbed her eyes, then replaced the spectacles. 'Maybe there's a clash of personalities. Nevertheless for your own good you should try to fit in wherever possible. I know it can sometimes be difficult.' She gave a small smile. 'In the circumstances you'll be glad to know you'll be transferred to Casualty for the next few months. Then you'll have done a period in each department.'

Emma felt a wave of sheer delight. No more to be under Sister Darling and to be in the department she had long wanted made the future look much brighter.

'I advise you to study hard for your examinations. I know some nurses join an agency to earn more money in their spare time, but I strongly recommend that you devote yourself to your studies. I believe you have the makings of a good nurse, but you have a long way to go. Now report to Sister Darling and she'll tell you when you'll be free to move to Casualty. Good morning, and good luck.'

Emma thanked her and went out into the corridor with a light heart. She glanced at the time. If she went straight back to her ward her coffee break would be lost for ever, so she ran happily down the stairs and out into the grounds. There was a covered way to the canteen in case the weather was bad, but Emma was glad to have a breath of fresh air, although it wasn't all that fresh but dust-laden as the wind blew in from the direction of the main road.

She looked around the canteen to see if there was someone there she knew, but there was no one. A hospital with a thousand nurses, and you never seemed to arrive there at the same time as your friends, seemed incredible but true. She took her coffee to a table beside a window which overlooked the car park. No matter what the time of day it was always full and she could not

believe all the cars belonged to the staff or visitors, but
were probably left there by people who worked in the
vicinity. Then she saw what she had really been looking
for. The silver-grey Porsche snaked up and parked in
Nigel's place. With a lift of her heart she saw him get
out and look around for a moment as if he too had been
wanting a breath of fresh air before disappearing into
the hospital for the rest of the day. The breeze ruffled
his hair and blew the wayward strand over his
forehead—and dust into his eye, apparently, for he
fiddled with it before crossing to the hospital entrance.
With a smile of satisfaction she knew that not only
would she be away from Sister Darling's carping in
future but that Nigel would be working in Casualty
more often than on the ward.

She drained her cup, pushed back her chair and made
her way to the ward, she hoped for the last time. She
might have known. When she reached the Sister's office
Nigel was already there, and she would have to wait
until he had gone before telling Sister Darling of her
move. Slipping hurriedly past her door, she joined
Nurse Brown to see what needed to be done.

'Heavens, I thought you'd done a bunk. What am I
supposed to do? Go for coffee or an early lunch?' she
grumbled.

'Sorry, Judy, but I had to see the SNO and she kept
me. You hurry along now.'

'The SNO? What did she want? Judy's eyes were wide
with curiosity.

'I'll tell you later. Hush! Here comes trouble.'

Emma hurried to join Sister Darling and Nigel. The
Sister gave her a hard, sharp look, but her voice was
superficially sweet.

'It's nice to see you back, Nurse Glover. I thought
perhaps you'd left us. Please prepare Miss Lucey for
Doctor.'

Emma did as she was told, then glanced up at Nigel

with a smile which he completely ignored. After their
journey and lovely meal together and their friendly
conversation; after their cancelled outing and the ticket
he had given her for her return journey, she would have
thought he could have smiled or said 'Good morning.'
She glared at him resentfully, and quite unexpectedly he
turned to look at her, and a look of surprise spread over
his face at her ferocity. She tried to turn it into a smile,
but it was too late, his attention had switched to his
patient.

Drat the man! Couldn't she get it into her stupid head
to stop thinking about him? Stop caring whether he
spoke to her or not? For the rest of his round she
avoided him as much as possible, and for the first time
ever was glad when he left the ward and she was able to
speak to Sister Darling.

'May I have a word, please, Sister?' she asked.

'If you must. Come in and close the door. Now what
is it?'

Emma stood humbly before Sister's desk for what she
hoped would be the last time. Unable to completely hide
her pleasure, she said triumphantly, 'Miss Gow told me
I'm moving to Casualty to complete my training, so
when will I be free to go there, please?'

Sister Darling looked almost as pleased as Emma did
herself. 'Good. Let me warn you that you'll need to
keep on your toes there, it's a busy department. They
won't be keen on having a nurse whose thoughts are
constantly three hundred miles away, they can't do with
slackers.'

Hot words of indignation fought to be spoken, but
Emma pushed them aside. What would be the use?
Sister Darling would always get the better of her, and all
she would do was upset herself.

'I think I'll enjoy it, Sister,' she said amiably.

'But will they enjoy having you there?' Sister scanned
her roster. 'Report to Casualty at two o'clock. I daresay

we can struggle along without you after that,' she added
sarcastically.

'I hope so, Sister, and thank you,' said Emma,
determinedly pleasant.

Emma expected no good wishes for the future or
regret at losing her, and got none. What she did get was
a curt nod of dismissal and a command to close the door
after her.

Nurse Brown looked at her questioningly. 'What's
going on? First the SNO and now Sister. What's it all
about?'

'I'm moving to Casualty to complete my training,'
Emma told her. 'You've already done that, haven't
you?'

'Yes, thank the Lord, it's horrible down there, quite
different from here.'

'Horrible? In what way?' Emma asked in dismay.

Nurse Brown pulled a face. 'Oh—accidents, fights,
strokes, death—you name it and you get it there. And
the sister isn't like Sister Darling.'

'How do you mean?' Emma stared at her.

'Well, you'd never get two like her, she's the most
wonderful Sister, a good disciplinarian who knows
everything about each patient and seems to have second
sight about anything that's worrying them. I think she's
super.'

Emma blinked. 'You are talking about Sister
Darling?'

Nurse Brown looked her up and down. 'Of course I
am, and I'm not the only one who thinks highly of
her—you've only got to watch Dr Shaw when he's with
her, you can tell he thinks the sun shines out of her.'

'I've never thought of her like that,' Emma said
shortly.

'How do you see her then?'

'Well, she's always finding fault and—and her
manner is quite different to us when a doctor is

present, she's all sweetness then.'

'Of course she finds fault, that's her job. And naturally her manner is different when a doctor is present, because she's considerate, she doesn't want to embarrass us.'

'Oh, is that what it is? You could have fooled me. Anyway, I shall be delighted to get away.'

'Gossiping again, Nurse Glover? Let me assure you I shall be even more delighted to see you go.' Sister Darling had suddenly appeared beside them like the evil witch in a pantomime. Emma had neither heard nor seen anyone arrive, and now she wondered guiltily how much of their conversation she had overheard. Had Nurse Brown been aware of Sister's presence, and was that why she had been speaking so highly of her?

Emma began to wonder whether maybe she was more to blame than Sister Darling. Was she as irritating to Sister as Sister was to her? Had she started off in the ward on the wrong foot? A suspicion sneaked into her mind. Was it possible that Sister was envious of her relationship with Nigel? Whatever the reson it was too late to overcome it now. She would start afresh and more cautiously in Casualty.

She hardly knew what she ate for lunch, and at two o'clock sharp she presented herself to Sister Telford in Casualty. She was a large, capable-looking woman with a serious, harassed expression. She glanced briefly at Emma and asked what she wanted.

'I'm Nurse Glover, Sister, and I've been sent here to do my last few months' training.'

A look of relief softened the lines on the Sister's face. 'Then I'm very glad to see you, Nurse. We can do with all the help we can get, we've been short-staffed for some time. Normally you would be off duty at two-thirty, so I suggest you look around the department and acquaint yourself with where things are kept and how things are done here, then get along home.'

'Thank you, Sister, but if you're busy I'm quite willing to stay on for a while,' Emma said.

The Sister smiled her appreciation. 'Thank you, but no. I shall expect to see you at eight o'clock sharp in the morning.' With a friendly smile she turned away to answer a call.

Emma felt as if she were on a busy railway station after a major accident. Trolleys were manoeuvred to make way for even more; doctors scrubbed up at sinks; others held up X-rays to the light; curtains on cubicles were whisked to and fro and patients waited anxiously in makeshift bandages for attention. Telephones rang; children cried; men swore and there was a babble of voices. Emma's heart swelled. Tomorrow she was going to be a part of this. As for today, she realised she was getting in people's way, and very soon she decided to take Sister's advice and head for home.

CHAPTER SEVEN

EMMA WAS IN Casualty before eight o'clock the next morning, eager to get started. To her surprise there was only one patient awaiting attention, a workman who had fallen off his motorbike. He was in the dressings room waiting for the X-ray pictures to show the extent of his injuries, a suspected fractured clavicle.

When Emma had introduced herself to the nurse on duty she said, 'I'm amazed. I thought that in Casualty I'd be run off my feet.'

Nurse Seymour gave a wry smile. 'Wait until you go off duty before you make a remark like that! It's somewhat premature.'

'Oh, I see. So this is the quietest time of the day?'

Molly Seymour shrugged. 'Who can tell? We get a fair number of RTAs early mornings, people like you who are eager to get to work!'

Emma laughed. 'I'm not always guilty of that. In fact I can't remember it ever having happened before. But I was so glad to get off Women's Medical and I felt like a born-again nurse.'

'I quite liked that ward when I was on it.'

'Were you under Sister Darling? Emma asked cautiously.

'No, she came when I left.'

'Lucky you!'

'Was she a so-and-so, then?'

'That's putting it politely! Whose place am I taking here? Somebody wonderfully proficient?'

'Not so's you'd notice. It was Jenny Ford. Did you know her?'

Emma shook her head.

'If something could be dropped Jenny would drop it, preferably in front of a bad-tempered doctor. She was nervous as a kitten.'

'Poor girl, I know the feeling,' Emma said ruefully. 'Not that I've ever been particularly nervous, but if you know someone has got it in for you it makes you do things wrong. Maybe that *is* being nervous.'

'I know what you mean, but Jenny wasn't cut out to be a nurse,' said Nurse Seymour.

'That's tough. So where has she gone now? God help her if it's Women's Medical.'

'No, she's cleared out.'

'You mean she's left nursing?' Emma stared at her wide-eyed.

'Yes, and I think it was a wise decision. I believe the SNO had a word in her ear.'

Emma looked appalled. 'So she's out of work?'

'No, she's taking a course to become a nanny and I think she'd be very suited to that. Miss Gow gave her a letter of recommendation to a well-known training school.'

'That sounds super. What a good idea. Would you like that?'

Molly gave a shout of dismay. 'Not on your life! I'm not all that keen on kiddywinks. Having said that, I think I'd be batty about my own.'

Sister Telford came hurriedly from her office. 'There's a multiple RTA. Ambulances are on their way with four stretcher cases, two with severe head injuries. Alert the team, please.'

Almost immediately the department was alive with doctors, their white coats flying, and nurses who seemed to appear from nowhere. Soon the ambulances zoomed up to the entrance doors, and Emma and Nurse Seymour hurried forward to meet them. An unconscious girl was taken straight through to the resuscitation room.

'What happened?' Molly asked the ambulance man.

'She was driving a Mini and a van skidded across the road in front of her and she couldn't stop.'

'Was she alone in the car?'

He shook his head. 'A couple of kiddies were in the back.'

Emma looked uneasily at the other stretchers. 'Where are they?'

'They weren't badly hurt, they came in another ambulance.'

Sister Telford, who was here, there and everywhere, said, 'Nurse Glover, take this blood for cross-matching, please, and tell the radiographers that Mr Wilks is on his way and will want to see the films right away.'

The other patient with serious head injuries was a middle-aged man who had been sitting in the van when the crash happened. The small van was a write-off.

As Emma trudged up the two flights of stairs to the Path Lab for what seemed the umpteenth time she wondered why it wasn't situated near Casualty. Granted there were lifts to the second floor, but they took ages to arrive and moved slowly and reluctantly both when opening the doors and transporting you aloft.

The driver of the skidding van had come off lightly and only needed a tetanus injection and some stitches in a leg wound. Emma saw Nigel going into the cubicle to do the suturing. She moved forward eagerly hoping to assist, but Linda Chapman was already there. Emma pictured him bending over the man's leg, his lovely eyes intent on his work. She wondered whether he was good at 'needlework', as they called it, and guessed that he must be, because he was so careful not to hurt people's feelings, she had seen that by his attitude to Derek, so he would have practised and practised suturing until he was proficient.

She realised she was cleaning wounds and applying sterile dressings automatically and knew she must concentrate on what she was doing, although it was difficult when Nigel was in the vicinity. When she judged that he would have finished dealing with his patient she hurried outside her cubicle hoping to see him, but he had gone, and she felt cheated. She returned to her patient, put a tubi-gauze covering on his leg and told him he was free to leave.

'Make an appointment for Friday, but come back sooner if it causes you concern,' she told him.

As the hours passed they were continually busy with the expected crop of sprains and cuts, strokes and heart attacks, but Emma enjoyed every minute.

When she reached her flat she flopped into a chair and sipped a cup of hot water with a tea-bag in it. For the first time she really sympathised with Dorothy when she said her legs wouldn't let her go out on the town when she came off duty. She was worried about Dorothy doing agency work as well as her ordinary duties. She could not imagine having a holiday abroad would be worth all that, she would be so exhausted she would not be able to enjoy it. Better to buy a sun-ray lamp and stay at home.

Her legs might be feeling tired and her head fuzzy, but Emma knew she must do some studying. Getting out lecture notes and textbooks, she forced herself to take in what she was reading and jot down salient points for easy revision later on. She found the theoretical side of nursing far more difficult that the practical, but realised its importance.

Celia arrived and seemed inclined to chat. Emma stifled a groan. That girl could go for weeks on end giving you no more than a grunt or monosyllabic reply, and now when Emma wanted silence she began to speak.

'How are you liking Casualty?' she asked.

'Very much so far, but it's awfully tiring, didn't you find that?'

'Yes, but I don't mind if it's interesting work. But my favourite department is Medical, either men's or women's.'

'Where do you go next?'

'Intensive Care. You have to be on your toes there—you can't let your mind wander or drop off during the night.'

'I didn't know we had to do IC I understood when I'd finished in Casualty I'd done the lot.'

'So you have. I stayed on an extra year for Intensive Care becuase I'm going out to Malawi to do missionary work.'

Emma really looked at Celia for the first time. She had learned more about her in the last few minutes than all the time she'd shared with her.

'Missionary work? That's a very worthy cause. What made you decide you wanted to do it?'

Celia looked down her nose and Emma realised the gesture which she had thought was one of disapproval was in reality shyness. She lifted her shoulders awkwardly. 'We've had some very interesting speakers from Malawi in our church and they made me feel I should do what I can for the deprived people in the world. And—well—' she dug her heel in the carpet and looked thoroughly uncomfortable, 'actually I'm—I'm getting—married.'

'Married!' Emma felt that now she had heard everything. 'Congratulations. Why haven't we heard any of this before?'

'Well, you know what Dorothy is, she'd have made it seem——'

Emma knew just what she meant.

'What does your boyfriend think about you going abroad? Won't he mind?'

Celia looked surprised. 'Oh no. Oh—you see, he's in the Church and he's going there too—as a teacher.'

'Why, that's lovely,' Emma said heartily. 'When will you be leaving?'

'Not—not for several months. We've both got to finish our training and take a course in missionary work too.'

'How exciting to be having a new life completely and a husband and see life in another country!'

Emma felt a twinge of envy and guilt. When she herself had thought of going abroad to see life outside a hospital she had thought of going entirely for pleasure; helping the deprived had not entered her head. She was so interested in Celia's news that she knew she could do no more studying tonight.

'Shall I get us something to eat?' she asked.

'No, thanks, there was a sausage sizzle at church, so I'm pretty full.'

'Lucky you!'

Unwilling to cook just for herself, Emma beat up an egg and had it in milk, comforting herself by thinking she had all the goodness without the work of cooking it some other way.

They were busy on Friday morning when a young policeman arrived in Casualty carrying a blue bundle in his arms. He made his way to Sister Telford's office. After a moment or two the sister emerged and catching Emma's eye beckoned to her.

Emma hurried over. 'Yes, Sister?'

'Take baby and keep her warm while I prepare for her in the baby care unit. She's suffering from hypothermia and needs to be re-warmed gradually. Body heat is best for her at the moment.'

Emma took her from the Sister. 'Poor little mite! What's happened?'

'She was found naked in a plastic bag beside a rubbish dump. Don't waste any time, Nurse.'

Emma fetched a 'space' blanket to replace the
policeman's jacket in which he had wrapped her. She
returned it to him with a smile. He looked down at the
baby.

'I'll call in, see how she's getting on.'

When he had gone Emma pulled off her apron,
opened the bodice of her dress and held the icy-cold
baby next to her body, murmuring endearments. She
prayed that she might live and willed her body to give
out all the heat she needed. There seemed hardly any
signs of life, but the wonder of the tiny features, the
scrappy eyebrows, the fine down of hair, filled Emma
with a flood of maternal love. She was so intent on her
precious bundle that she only vaguely heard a voice
summoning her.

'Nurse! Nurse!'

'You poor little darling,' she murmured. 'You're
so beautiful, how could anyone leave you like
that?'

'For heaven's sake don't stand there looking at
nothing! Will you please assist me?' an irate voice
demanded.

Emma looked up, a bemused expression in her eyes,
to see Nigel striding angrily towards her. As he
drew closer he looked down at her, then looked
again.

'I—I didn't realise it was you, Emma. What have
you——' He stopped. 'Good God, where did that come
from?' He peered down at the child.

'She was left naked in a plastic bag and Sister told
me to give her body warmth while she's preparing for
her.'

His face became tender. 'Poor little scrap! I'm sorry I
shouted at you, I didn't know——'

Emma smiled up at him. 'No, of course you didn't.'

There was a click and they both looked around. A
group of press photographers raised their thumbs and

winked in appreciation of a good picture.

'God, they turn up everywhere! They must have some seventh sense,' Nigel frowned.

Sister Telford bustled up to them, breathing heavily. 'No, they come here every morning in the hope of getting something for their paper. They have their job to do the same as we have, I don't object to them coming.'

She lifted the edge of the blanket and studied the baby's face, then she nodded. 'Bring baby along, Nurse, and we'll get her fixed up.'

The day continued to be busy, and Emma wondered whether there could be any household in the neighbourhood where at least one of its members was not involved in some mishap. Before going off duty she went up to the baby care unit, almost afraid to ask how 'her' baby was doing.

The nurse in charge was optimistic. 'Her temperature has risen a little, which is a good sigh, but it's asking a lot, and we can only hope. She's quite a good weight, and that helps.'

On the way home Emma bought an evening paper, wondering whether there would be any mention of it. As she turned the pages she saw a large picture of herself with the buttons of her bodice undone, holding the baby close, and she was smiling at Nigel, who had the most wonderful, tender expression on his face. The picture was over the story,

Loving Tender care from a dedicated nurse and doctor. Nurse Glover and Dr Shaw with the abandoned baby girl hospital staff have called Emma after Nurse Glover who is holding her. The baby was found naked in a plastic bag beside a rubbish dump by a schoolboy on his way to school. 'I thought it was a kitten,' he said. 'If it had been a boy I'd have liked them to call it Roger after me.'

An article on the plight of the unmarried mother followed, but Emma didn't read that right away. She was staring instead at Nigel, looking so kind, so handsome. It was a lovely picture.

When she got off the bus she bought another newspaper so that she could send one home. She wondered gleefully what Sister Darling would make of it, and knew she would not be pleased that her 'doppy rustic' was shown in such a good light, and with Nigel too.

On the TV news the affair was reported briefly and a plea was made for the mother to come forward as she would probably be in need of medical attention.

Emma felt desperately sorry for the girl and what she must have suffered both mentally and physically. Worst of all would be never to hold your baby in your arms, see it crawl or hear it say its first words. She hoped the mother would come forward, but she doubted it. To leave it unclothed and by a rubbish dump was so heartless, likening it to trash. What sort of a girl would do that? A chilling thought came into her mind. Maybe it had been left by an uncaring boyfriend or irate father. Poor, poor girl!

To take her mind off the matter she began to study. Much later she heard the door open and wondered where she was. Only then did she realise she had fallen asleep. So much for her studies!

Dorothy came in looking weary. 'You been asleep? Lucky you, I wish I had.' She gave a tired smile. 'You're the talk of the town, you with your topless picture splashed all over the paper. Everyone said it ought to be on page three.' She yawned widely. 'You make a smashing-looking couple—or trio, I suppose. Could have been your baby and Dr Shaw's if it had a different story underneath. I bet someone will cut it out and pin it on the notice board. Good job you're not working with Sister Darling.' She yawned again. 'I'm dead on my feet! Do I need to get undressed?'

Emma packed away her books and got ready for bed. Before she went to sleep she looked at the picture again and wished she might dream of it. But wishes seldom come true.

CHAPTER EIGHT

EVERY EVENING Emma did her studying and ticked off the days on her calendar until the date of the examinations. The third-year students were advised to apply to other hospitals for any advertised vacancies, although it was understood that acceptance would be subject to the results. They were warned that there would only be a few vacancies for staff nurses at Nightingale's.

Emma had already applied to St Joseph's in Cornwall where Nigel was hoping to go. If he was there that was where she wanted to be. But she guessed that vacancies at St Joseph's would be in great demand, so she also applied to Meadowsweet in Somerset, because she wanted to be somewhere in the West Country.

Celia was studying hard too, but Dorothy, busy with her agency work, seemed to have neither the time nor the energy to do so.

'Is it worth doing that extra work when your exams are so important?' Emma asked anxiously.

Dorothy rested her head on her arms. 'No, I don't think it is. Heather seems to be taking it in her stride and I'd love to go on this holiday, but I don't think I can keep going, I get so tired.'

Emma put her hand on her shoulder. 'You've got the rest of your life to take a holiday abroad, but your exams are now. Get your promotion and you'll be able to take an exotic holiday with a clear conscience.'

'I probably won't pass them anyway,' Dorothy sighed.

'That's nonsense and you know it. Everyone says

you're an excellent nurse,' Emma said warmly.

'I know I'm OK on the practical work, it's the theoretical that gets me down.'

'Nearly all of us feel that way. Do give up that extra work, Dorothy, and we'll study together. We can ask each other questions. I've taken a lot of notes. So what about it?'

Dorothy made no reply, and Emma glanced at her sharply. Her mouth was sagging open and her breathing heavy. Emma went to her anxiously, then smiled. Dorothy was already asleep.

Emma knew she would be sorry to leave Casualty at Nightingale's when she had to move on. She loved meeting the patients who had come in off the streets and attending to their needs. It was a very busy department, probably the busiest in the hospital, and frequently Emma could not believe it was time to go off duty.

Although she was so busy she found time each day to go to the baby care unit, and it was with pride and delight that she saw 'her' baby gradually picking up strength, there was a little colour in her cheeks and more energy in her movements. Sister Balmain thought all the babies were beautiful, and Emma agreed. But like a fond mother Emma knew none of them could equal 'hers' for beauty and perfection.

Today she had not had a minute to spare, but she promised herself she would pay a visit when she went off duty. As she was about to leave Casualty a porter wheeled in an elderly man who was having a stroke. His wife, who accompanied him, was distraught.

'He was quite all right, we were talking and laughing, and he just fell down. He isn't having a stroke—they're wrong, he must have stumbled and fallen. He couldn't get up because his legs haven't been good for a long time and he's too heavy for me to lift. But that's all. It isn't a stroke, is it?' She looked pleadingly from her husband to Emma.

'Doctor will come right away and find out for sure. You just sit here and I'll fetch you a cup of tea.' Emma fetched the sweetened tea and sat beside her, talking as comfortingly as she could. 'Don't worry too much, it may be a very mild stroke if it is one.'

When his wife seemed calmer Emma went to Sister Telford and told her she was going off duty. Then she took the lift to the baby care unit. She tapped on the door, as protocol did not permit her to go in uninvited.

When the door opened Emma smiled at Sister Balmain. 'I'm a bit late, I was held up in Casualty. Did you think I'd forgotten baby Emma? How is she today?'

'Come in, dear.' Sister Balmain laid a large comforting hand on her shoulder. 'I know this will come as a shock, but despite the improvement baby was making—you knew the cards were stacked against her, didn't you, dear?'

Emma felt as if a cold hand had been laid on her heart. 'Yes—but——' She glanced desperately over the Sister's shoulder to the cot where Nigel stood. 'But what's the trouble?'

'I'm sorry, dear, I'm afraid she just slipped away from us in the last few minutes.'

'No, oh no!' Emma wailed. Pulling herself from the Sister's restraining arm, she rushed across the ward, pushing aside the doctor who was gently covering the baby's face with the sheet. She dragged it back. As she saw the tiny, inanimate face tears of anguish scalded her eyes and cascaded down her cheeks. Dr Shaw took both her hands in one of his and with the other replaced the sheet. She looked up at him with angry resentment, about to protest at what had happened, eager to blame somebody, then she saw the cold, hard expression on his face and was silenced.

'I want to speak to you in my office, Nurse,' he said in a clipped voice.

Emma had no wish to speak to anybody, nor did she have to. 'I'm off duty,' she said defiantly, in a choked voice.

'At once, Nurse,' he said authoritatively, as if she had not spoken.

She fumbled in her pocket for a tissue, without success, so she furtively dabbed her eyes with the corner of her apron, as she followed him blindly.

He closed the door of his office behind her, then sat behind his desk and eyed her for a moment. Then he said in a voice so distant she could scarcely recognise it,

'How long have you been training, Nurse?'

The stupid man! He knew damn well she was shortly going to take her exams, and what had that to do with him, anyhow?

'N-nearly three years,' she mumbled, and wiped her cheek with the back of her hand.

'Then isn't it time you took a grip of yourself? I take it you're hoping to qualify, or are you opting out of the profession?'

Emma saw him through a blur of tears, saw light brown eyes with green and yellow flecks in them. She wondered why she had ever thought they were lovely. They were hard and the flecks in them like stone chippings, and they looked as if they belonged to some ferocious animal who was just about to pounce on you and maul you to death.

'Of course I'm hoping to qualify, I'm not taking the exams for fun,' she said rudely, and didn't care.

'Then let me tell you I hope you don't qualify. A nurse needs to be someone with enough strength of character to tend people who are sick to the utmost of their ability, with empathy, or course, but never to

become emotionally involved. Unfortunately a patient
may die, that's the way it is. But there are other patients
who need care and attention from a nurse who is
concerned with their welfare, not one whose mind is
on a patient who has died. We can't all go around
weeping, you know, no matter how much we would like
to.'

She hated him. How could he be so unfeeling when
that darling baby lay lifeless? He was hard-hearted and
horrible!

'Some people are more unfeeling than others,' she
said, glaring at him.

'If that's your attitude I strongly recommend you
to think very carefully about your future, ask yourself whether nursing is the right career for
you.'

How dared he speak to her like that! Anyone would
think he was the hospital's chief consultant. If she felt
like crying he couldn't stop her. In fact she couldn't
stop herself, and tears rained down her face. She tried to
wipe them away with her hands, but it was hopeless.
Barely stifling a sigh, Nigel took a handful of tissues
from a box on his desk and passed them to her.

'Run along,' he said, as if she were a troublesome
child.

Emma fled to the wash-room and splashed cold water
on her face. She felt sad, weary and disillusioned, and it
was some time before she felt calm enough to make her
way home.

Ignoring for once the creaking of Mrs Clay's door as
she peeped through the crack, and deaf to the shouting
and rowing of other tenants, she let herself into her flat,
then lay down on her bed. She had lost everything that
mattered. She could still feel the tiny cold body pressed
against her chest; see the gossamer eyelashes; the
strands of hair that lay bravely on the scalp and the
microscopic fingernails, and she ached with longing.

Little Emma had been getting on so well, why couldn't she have lived? And why hadn't Nigel understood and sympathised with how she felt instead of being so horrible?

She went to her writing case and took out the newspaper cutting to look once again at the baby she held. She glanced at herself and Nigel, and was hurt anew by the tender, loving expression on his face, which she now knew was just a façade. She thought she had known him. He treated patients who exaggerated or feigned illness with icy disdain, but if they were genuinely ill or worried he was unbelievably kind, gentle and reassuring, oblivious to the fact that maybe he had been working long hours and should have gone off duty long before. He had been kind to her too, giving her a lift home when he had no reason to do so. Then there was Derek. Who else did she know who would have understood the situation and dealt with it so tactfully? It all went to show that he was neither hard-hearted nor uncaring, so why had be behaved so out of character today?

Then gradually she understood, and her hurt began to lessen. Oh, it was an old hackneyed epxression, but on this occasion she believed it fitted. He had been cruel to be kind. He had forced her to think back over her training, when you were warned never to become emotionally involved with a patient or you would not survive. A nurse had to be strong and hide her feelings, for what would the staff and the patients think if Nigel, for example, were to dissolve into tears when they lost a patient? There were procedures to be gone through, relatives to be comforted, other patients to attend to and, if you were married, your own family to consider. He had been so clever. If he had sympathised with her, maybe dried her tears, said soothing words, she would never have learned how to behave. She sighed heavily. It was going to be very difficult, but he was quite right, she must learn to control her emotions or leave the profession.

She wondered, not for the first time, if she was really suited to be a nurse. She thought of other vocations. How would it be working in Reception or Records? She would be in the hospital atmosphere—but it wouldn't be the same, the people would merely be names. Now if she were to work in an office or shop she would know what hours she would be working, and would only have an occasional awkward customer or boss to contend with. But no, despite all the drawbacks, nursing was what she wanted to do and she was stuck with it. If she passed her exams. Before she started on her studying she needed to have something to eat.

She put away the cutting and tried to put her sad thoughts away too. Then she bathed and changed into her warm quilted housecoat and went into the kitchen to see what she could rustle up. There was not much to choose from as they all usually ate in the canteen. There was some bread, a piece of hard cheese and a couple of tomatoes. Emma cut the green away from the cheese and sliced the tomato and toasted it under the grill. When it was cooked she made a cup of coffee. She felt stronger when she had eaten and more able to face her studying.

Then at last it was the night before the exams. She and Dorothy had spent several hours recently testing each other's knowledge in preparation for the great day, and Emma believed there could not possibly be a question for which they had no answer. They sat facing each other on the hard chairs.

'It's your turn to ask me. I'm not too hot on the urological scene, so pick something from that,' Emma said wearily.

'Righto.' Dorothy turned some pages, muttered,

'We've done that,' then said, 'Here we are. Give me four causes of chronic renal failure.'

Emma wrinkled her forehead and stared into space. 'Well, there's—um—pyelo-nephritis and—polycystic kidneys. And—oh, heck!—oh, I know, malignant hypertension. Malignant hypertension,' she repeated. 'Four, you say?' She shook her head. 'I'm hanged if I can think of anything else.'

'Glomerulo-nephritis. And if you can spell that you're a better man than I am. Here, you'd better copy it down.' Dorothy pushed the book across.

'Thanks,' said Emma when she had copied it. 'Now I suppose you want a question. Here's a beauty for you. What is Ankylosing Spondylitis and what are the symptoms?'

'Oh, it's an inflammatory disease—it's mostly young men who get it. Don't ask me why.'

'Go on, then, tell me the symptoms.'

'The symptoms? How should I know, I haven't had it.'

'God willing, we won't have any of these awful complaints, but we're supposed to know about them. So do you want me to tell you?'

'No. They get spinal rigidity and limitation of chest expansion.'

'Who's a clever clogs!' Emma threw the book on the table. 'There's so much I don't know, but I'm not going to study any more tonight. If I fail I'll throw in the sponge and know it isn't the right job for me. There must be plenty of things you can do where they pay the earth and you don't have to do any studying.'

'If there is then lead me to it. I can't say I've heard of any like that,' said Dorothy.

Emma looked dreamily into the one-bar fire. 'It must have been lovely once upon a time to get married at eighteen and never have to work. To spend your days lying on a hammock or a chaise-longue reading novels and eating chocolates.'

'And getting as fat as a pig,' Dorothy put in.

'Funny, they never used to. In my picture books the women always looked frail and slender.'

'Huh! They were pictured like that for the benefit of kids. In fact they were pregnant most of the time. And they died young or were permanent invalids, and I wouldn't much like that. But anyway, who'd want to return to those days? If you think of the hardships! No electricity, so no household gadgets to make life easier. Probably outside loos and water. And whichever stratum of society you happened to be in the man was the lord and master. Blow that for a life!'

'I know. It's funny how things have changed in a comparatively short time. I can't understand why girls married those awful bossy men, can you?'

'The alternative wasn't any better. You'd have been dependent on your father and he was just such another. Dog's life, wasn't it?'

'Mm. But I'd hate to marry a wimp.'

Dorothy's eyelids dropped but couldn't quite hide the mischievous glint in her eyes. 'I know who you fancy, but you're wasting your time.'

Emma stared at her in amazement. 'Who *I* fancy? Then you know more than I do,' she protested.

'But Sister Darling is the one who'll get him, isn't she?' Dorothy said slyly.

The colour flooded Emma's cheeks and her eyes flashed. 'You talk a lot of rubbish. I'm off to bed, and you don't deserve to be wished good luck tomorrow. But if I don't it will be on my conscience.'

'And good luck to you too,' said Dorothy, and yawned widely.

CHAPTER NINE

SLEEP HAD been a mockery. The few disjoined hours when Emma slept had been like nightmares, with voices getting louder and louder demanding answers to questions which made no sense. Large forbidding faces, each a caricature of Sister Darling, came closer and closer and shouted, 'You've failed! You've failed!'.

She reared up in sudden panic when her alarm sounded. With a sigh of relief she silenced it and got out of bed, glad the night was over and hoping she would feel a new person after she had showered, but she didn't. Maybe breakfast would give her strength? She was never to know, for her throat refused to co-operate.

She was not alone in her misery. Celia looked a pale shade of yellow and turned from the thought of tea and toast with a shudder. Dorothy was paler and puffier than usual and her red-rimmed eyes watered over the smoke from her cigarette.

'We ought to try and eat something,' Emma said half-heartedly, thinking of the long morning ahead.

The other two stared at her as if she had said something obscene and made no attempt to follow her advice. She poured herself some tea, took a sip, choked and threw the rest away. Annoyed with the weakness of her body, she came to the conclusion that exams were bad for your health and should come with a government warning.

They set off for the hospital together in comparative silence. There they met up with other candidates who appeared in no better shap than themselves. There were just a few who laughed and spoke louder than usual to convince themselves and others they were not in the least nervous.

Emma checked that she had the things she might need. Three ballpoint pens because she knew from experience that they had a nasty habit of drying up in emergencies; paper tissues in case she was overcome by emotion and a tube of peppermints because her mouth was apt to behave like her pens.

A bell sounded and the doors to the examination room were wedged open. The candidates trooped in, seemingly eager now to get started on the list of questions which lay face downwards on each desk. Emma checked her watch with the clock on the wall and saw there were two minutes to go. The invigilators came in, murmured a few words to each other, then as the minute hand on the clock jumped forward to the hour the doors were closed. There was a moment's hush and then the chief invigilator spoke in a calm, pleasant voice.

'Good morning, students. You have two hours in which to answer your questions, during which time silence must be observed. If there is a question which you feel unable to answer you would do well to leave it until later and go back to it if you have time. I wish you all well.' She paused for a second. 'You may turn your papers over now. Thank you.'

There was a rustle of movement, throats were cleared and seats were shifted. At first Emma's eyes blurred, then when they had cleared she saw the first question was comparatively simple, and she felt grateful to the examiners, because it was a relief to be able to get started.

All in all Emma was not displeased with her effort; indeed, some of the questions were those she and Dorothy had set each other, but she had scarcely finished writing when time was up and pens had to be laid down. Some students who were either sure to pass or certain to fail had finished writing and leaned back in their seats some time before, causing others to panic and write frantically in an effort to catch up with them.

A bell rang and the papers were collected, and the students were free until the next day when they would have their practical examination. Now they trooped into the canteen comparing answers, pleased by some and groaning at others. Emma and Dorothy managed to sit together.

Dorothy seemed quietly confident. 'They were a doddle, weren't they?'

Emma looked at her wide-eyed. 'Do you think so? I agree some of them were all right, those questions we'd asked each other came up, that was a bit of luck. But what did you put for number five?'

If Dorothy was right—and Emma had no doubt she was—then she herself was wrong, and her spirits drooped. Oh, well, she had done her best. She ate cold ham and salad determinedly, more to keep up her strength then for enjoyment. Later on she realised that an afternoon spent with Dorothy was not a good idea. She went to bed early and when she awoke in the morning it was with surprise because she had slept for nine hours.

Nobody seemed as nervous for the practical examination. There was the feeling that if they had failed the theoretical they were done for anyhow.

Emma ate some cereal. 'Do you know who the examiner is?' she asked.

'Yes, Sister Tutor from Bart's—or is it Guy's? I'm not sure which,' Dorothy replied.

'Just her? I thought there was a panel?'

'There is, there are three altogether, one male and two female. I haven't heard who the others are, but they're probably from the General Nursing Council.'

For this examination each student had to demonstrate a procedure for a specific condition. One by one they were called in to the adjoining room where the three examiners sat. A student, acting as a patient, lay on a bed.

When it was Emma's turn she went in with a thumping heart. Her first question was, 'An elderly person has been admitted in a semi-conscious, drowsy condition, with cold and clammy skin. Will you give us your diagnosis and proposed treatment, please.'

'I would suspect hypothermia, especially if the extremities were blue. I would take the temperature and expect it to be below 35°C.'

She eyed the examiners calmly. There was yesterday's chief invigilator, who now seemed like an old friend; an elderly man who looked like a garden gnome with a mop of white hair and a beard to match, and a severe bespectacled middle-aged woman who Emma felt was the one to fear.

Yesterday's friend asked how she would take the patient's temperature.

'With a low-reading rectal thermometer, ma'am.'

The bespectacled woman put a trick question triumphantly. 'You would of course warm the patient as speedily as possible. How would you do this?'

Emma's thoughts flew to 'her' baby who had been admitted with hypothermia and for a moment she could think of nothing else. But they were awaiting her reply.

'No, ma'am, I would re-warm the patient gradually, as if it's done too quickly vasodilation would cause the blood pressure to drop and heat loss to increase.

The gnome nodded his head rapidly and beamed at her.

Apparently the interview was going too well for the severe woman. (Could it be Sister Darling in heavy disguise?) She had another go.

'Having ascertained that your patient is suffering from hypothermia and she is not too speedily warmed, are you then intending to leave her to her fate?'

'No, ma'am, I would cover her with an insulating space blanket and give her at least three litres of fluid to correct dehydration either by the oral route, a naso-gastric tube intravenously or rectally.'

The woman nodded grudgingly and there was a brief silence. The three of them whispered together, then Sister Tutor asked Emma if she had anything to add.

'I would keep a close watch on her readings and report any misgivings I had to the doctor in charge of the case,' Emma said.

She was pleased with her answers, which she knew were correct, thanks to the darling baby, because she had read up all about hypothermia at the time. There were more questions and a demonstration of inserting a naso-gastric tube in the poor 'model' student. Then she was free to go and it was all over, the studying, the doubts and the difficulties and the examinations. Whether she had passed or not, she vowed she would not go through it all again.

She was bobbing along the corridor on legs which felt they somehow did not belong to her when she saw Nigel approaching. Her heart, which she had thought would now beat steadily and calmly for evermore, proved how wrong she was by leaping like a flea. He looked so super, tall and broad as he strode along, his white coat streaming behind him, the lock of hair which insisted on falling over his forehead and—and then when he drew near he was looking directly at her with eyes that were of emerald-flecked amber set in gold.

He paused, and gave her a devastating smile. 'So it's D-Day today. How did it go?'

'Not—not too bad,' she said, wishing he was not so attractive, because she stumbled over her words when he was so close.

'Good. Glad they're over?'

'Rather!' she said fervently.

'And now you move on. Or are you hoping to stay here?'

She shook her head. 'I don't know what I shall be doing. My chief worry is whether I've passed.'

He smiled understandingly. 'It won't be long before you hear. Anyhow, good luck.'

He walked on, and Emma was very conscious of the curious glances of other nurses as they passed.

Talking to Nigel had made her feel even happier, and she went over the few words he said time and again. To celebrate the end of exams she went to the market and bought a bottle of sherry because she knew the three of them would have plenty to discuss tonight. When she reached her flat she even called out a friendly greeting to the ever-watchful Susan Clay, who poked out her head a fraction further from the door opening to tell Emma the postman had called.

Emma thanked her and laughed to herself. Susan missed nothing. It might be fun to discover what she would do if Dorothy, Celia and herself each arrived home with a man. Would she ring the police or stand with her ear pressed to the keyhole?

She was quite right. The postman had called, and there in the box were two letters, and they were both for Emma. On each envelope was stamped the name and address of a hospital authority. One was from Somerset and the other from Cornwall, both apparently in reply to her applications. Although she knew that an acceptance would be dependent upon exam results a refusal would dash her hopes completely. She looked at them doubtfully. Should she open them and maybe read the worst? But she couldn't leave them until tomorrow; she was too eager to know one way or the other.

She put them aside while she took off her coat and hat, then took the pins from her long nut-brown hair and brushed it, which always made her feel good. Then she opened the sherry and poured herself a drink to give herself Dutch courage and maybe ease her disappointment if she was turned down. Picking up the letters, she played a game with herself as to which she should open first. Eenie, meenie, minie, mo—she stopped and laughed, telling herself that she was quite mad. Then, closing her eyes, she picked up one of the letters and ripped it open. Only then did she see it was the one from Somerset.

She read it through and smiled. Her application was successful! But she pushed that aside as she reached for the other one. She read it through once and then again. Surely it was too good to be true? They too had provisionally accepted her. If only she had passed!

The future looked rosy. Cornwall was where Nigel was hoping to go, and she felt certain nobody would refuse his application. It would be great to be there where he was without having Sister Darling's eagle eye on them. And maybe—just maybe he would ask her to take him to Madron Wishing Well, and if he did, nothing and nobody would stop her this time. It was going to be wonderful. This must surely be the happiest day of her life. Unless—but she must not spoil it by considering failure.

Celia and Dorothy arrived together, a rare occurrence, drawn together with the mutual relief of exams being over.

'Thank God that's that,' said Dorothy as she pulled off her hat and coat.

Celia looked at her disapprovingly. 'I hope you mean that reverently, Dorothy.'

Emma gave an inward groan. Putting those two together was like having a cat and dog who disliked each other in the flat. She strove to bring a happy note into the atmosphere.

'Some sherry to celebrate, girls. Any takers?'

Dorothy picked up the bottle and glanced at the label. 'I suppose British sherry will have to do, but it always makes me feel I'm the sponge cake in the trifle,' she said.

'You look a bit like that too,' Emma retorted. 'There are some Epsom salts in the bathroom if you prefer. Which is it to be? How about you, Celia?'

'Thank you, Emma, I'll have sherry if I may. It was kind of you to buy it.' Celia gave Dorothy a reproving look.

They sat chatting and drinking and comparing answers until Emma could no longer keep her good news to herself. She took her letters from her handbag and waved them in the air.

'News, girls, news! Raise your glasses and drink to my good fortune. I've had acceptances for both my applications. How does that grab you?'

Only after she had spoken when she saw the expression on their faces did she realise she had been tactless, as they too had written to hospitals but not yet received replies. Not that it mattered to Celia, since she had already made her plans to go overseas, but she had to go through the motions in case there were any slip-ups.

'Lucky you,' she said now. 'Which will you go to?'

'Oh, Cornwall, that was my first choice.'

'That's St Joseph's, isn't it?' Dorothy asked.

'Yes, that's right.' Emma was surprised that she had heard of it.

Dorothy smiled into her sherry and wriggled her toes.

'Then I've got some good news and some bad news for you,' she said.

'Oh, I know! the hospital has burned down, I suppose,' Emma said drily.

Dorothy shook her head. 'Which do you want to hear first?'

Emma shrugged. 'The good news, I suppose.'

Dorothy stared at her with her pale blue heavy-lidded eyes. 'I heard that Dr Shaw was going there.'

Emma looked pleased but doubtful. 'I know he wanted to go there, but——'

'Apparently he was accepted, because they were all congratulating him.'

Now Emma was certain no day had ever brought her so much happiness. It would be a shame when she had to go to bed and bring it to an end.

Dorothy watched her carefully. 'Don't you want to hear the bad news?'

'Bad news? Oh, that.' She knew nothing could possibly mar her happiness now. 'OK, let's have it.'

'Well,' Dorothy savoured every word, 'I think they may have been congratulating him because Sister Darling——' She paused, placed a cigarette between her lips, fumbled in her handbag for her lighter and made several attempts to get it to work, while Emma waited anxiously for her to continue. At last she could wait no longer.

'Because Sister Darling what?' she prompted impatiently.

Dorothy drew on her cigarette, blew a spiral of smoke in the air, half-closed her eyes, had a fit of coughing, then said contendedly,

'Because Sister Darling is going there too.'

Emma looked at her with stricken eyes while happiness slithered away from her. 'Oh no!' she whispered.

'Now that's going to make it seem like home from home, isn't it?' Dorothy said smugly.

Emma felt a surge of anger. 'I shall never know. Don't forget I have an alternative. No way will I go to Cornwall if she's there. I shall go to Somerset, and I'm sure it's all for the best.'

She picked up her letters and went to her room. She sat on her bed and stared bleakly into space. She might have known her luck had been too good to last, and she should be grateful for the good things that had happened. But in her heart she knew that what had pleased her most had now gone, and what was left seemed of little importance. When she said going to Somerset might be for the best she had not meant it, but it was probably true, because Nigel and Sister Darling belonged to each other, and she herself would be wiser to keep away from him, otherwise she was courting unhappiness. With grim determination she took out her writing pad and wrote a letter of provisional acceptance to Somerset. Then, feeling as if she was tearing herself apart, she wrote annother to St Joseph's telling them that she was accepting a vacancy elsewhere. Now, while her mind was made up, she would post them and get it over and done with and try not to think of what might have been. But when she looked for her stamps she found she had run out. Never mind, tomorrow morning would do just as well.

Despite her day of excitement sheer weariness made her sleep long and heavily, and she awoke late. She dashed to the bathroom, dressed hastily and hurried into the kitchen, hoping she would have time for a cup of tea. Much to her surprise Dorothy was already there, eating toast and marmalade.

'Help yourself,' she said, pushing the toast and teapot towards her.

'Thanks. No time for toast, but I'm dying for some tea. What are you doing sitting here? Have you lost your job or your reason?'

Dorothy yawned. 'I'm on late shift today, so of
course I woke up early, didn't I? Always the way.'

Emma hurried to her room to pin up her hair and
change her shoes. Blast! She'd have no time to go to the
post office.

'Have you got any stamps?' she called.

'Any what?'

'Stamps—for my letters. I thought I had some.' She
hurried into the kitchen.

'I can get some,' Dorothy said without looking up
from her search for a cigarette.

'Thanks a lot if you'll post them. They're on the
mantelpiece. Be OK if I pay you tonight?'

Dorothy's grunt was her only reply. Emma ran
downstairs, opened the front door, tripped over the
broken step, recovered her balance and sped along the
road towards the bus stop, just managing to jump on as
the doors were closing.

'You didn't ought to do that, it's dangerous, and
I'm the one as'd get the blame,' the driver said
grumpily.

By running through the ambulance station, which was
not really allowed because it was often so busy that
pedestrians could be a hazard, Emma manged to reach
Casualty only a few minutes late.

But here was Sister Telford. 'I'm sorry I'm late,
Sister,' Emma said breathlessly.

'Celebrating too well last night, I suppose,' Sister
Telford said, her eyes twinkling.

Emma felt a great affection for this kind Sister who
got the best out of everybody without any of Sister
Darling's clock-watching, condemning manner. She
promised herself that if she ever became a Sister she
would model herself on Sister Telford.

'Resus!'

Immediately the cry went up the department became

vibrantly alive as white-coated figures and nurses ran into the resuscitation room, where there was all the latest equipment for saving life. Two coaches had collided on the motorway, other cars had smashed into them, and the casualties were being brought in by porters and nurses.

Some who were suffering only from shock and minor bruising were speedily dealt with, but others, less fortunate, were given pain-killing jabs and oxygen by the anaesthetist. The X-ray unit was wheeled in and Emma handed out quilted aprons as a protection against radiation. Radiographers produced pictures every few minutes which the doctors studied. Some patients were then taken to theatre, while others awaited admission to a ward which could take them. At the same time nurses and housemen attended to the routine arrivals. At long last, when all the motorway victims had been attended to, a strange peace descended on Casualty, despite the fact that it was as busy as usual.

As Emma removed Nigel's apron he heaved a sigh of relief. 'Thank goodness there were no fatalities,' he said with satisfaction.

'Not for the moment. But what about those who are in IC or had surgery? We don't know what will happen to them,' Emma said despondently.

He gave her a quick glance. 'I didn't know you were a pessimist.'

He didn't know anything about her, that was why. He didn't know that it would be a long time before she could look on the bright side of anything, now that her chance of going to St Joseph's and working near him had been dashed, thanks to Sister Darling.

'I hear you're going to St Joseph's where you wanted to go,' she said. 'Congratulatons.'

He frowned. 'Now how on earth do you know that? What is there about a hospital, that nothing can be kept secret?'

'It must be something in the air,' she smiled. 'I heard more than that. I heard Sister Darling is going there too.'

'Did you now? It's good to know that the grapevine can sometimes give out false information. Sister Darling is certainly not going to St Joseph's, she has her sights set higher. In fact she's been promoted to Administration—if you can call that promotion.'

'Has she? Has she really?' Emma's face was wreathed in a brilliant smile.

Nigel glanced at her knowingly. 'I'm sure she'd be very touched to know you were so pleased for her. I'll pass on your congratulations.'

Emma looked down guiltily, then up again. Was he teasing her? Didn't he know by now that she and Sister Darling were sworn enemies? He smiled and his green and gold eyes seemed to bore deep into her. Then he put his hand on her shoulder and squeezed it understandingly. She gave a shiver of delight and a look of sheer bliss spread across her face. She waited breathlessly, for she could see he was about to say something more, when his bleep sounded and he was called away.

The day slipped by. Every now and again Emma smiled happily to herself. She should surely have learned by now to take any information Dorothy passed on with a pinch of salt. Or had she told her that bit out of mischief? It was more than likely, and if Emma had not been feeling so happy she would have been after Dorothy's blood. Although she had been rushed off her feet for most of the day Emma gave up her seat on the bus to another woman, for happiness made her oblivious of tiredness.

As she swayed to and fro the driver braked suddenly and she was flung forward, saved from falling by another passenger. But that jerk had done more than throw her forward, it had jolted her memory, and with a sick feeling which started in her head, flooded her body and ended up like an iron fist on her heart she remembered her letter of refusal to St Joseph's. She clapped her hand over her mouth and stared desperately into space. The passenger who had saved her from falling now clutched at her sleeve.

'Are you all right? You take my seat, I'm getting off soon.'

Emma thanked her and sat in the proffered seat, glad to do so, because her legs felt weak. Curse Dorothy and curse herself for her impetuosity, there had been no need for her to reply so promptly, anger and disappointment had decided her. Now she had nothing to look forward to, just years and years of dull working days. She hoped she would have failed her exams and she could leave the hospital and never enter one again. A passenger touched her shoulder.

'Don't you get off here, ducks.'

Emma looked out of the window with bemused eyes, then rose hastily to her feet.

'Thanks very much.'

'I seen you most days and I thought you did. You 'ad a shock, dearie? You look a bit queer to me.'

'I'll be all right, thanks,' Emma called over her shoulder.

This was a horrible neighbourhood, the houses were in a dreadful state. A half-hearted effort had been made to improve her particular house, but in the attempt distemper and paint drips were splashed on the path and steps. The linoleum on the stairs was beginning to be dangerous from wear. Emma suppressed a shiver as Susan's door creaked open and she knew she was being watched. How she hated this place! It would be good to get away. If only it could have been to Cornwall!

She unlocked her door, hating the bleakness of the living room with its unwelcoming atmosphere. She had never got around to buying those cushions or lamps.

There was no more studying to be done, she had no letters to write, no particular book to read. She wished she had stayed behind and eaten in the canteen, anywhere was better than here. She decided to make a cup of tea, the panacea for all ills.

She glanced at the time, and there on the mantelpiece were the two letters Dorothy had forgotten to post. Emma stared at them in disbelief. Was this Dorothy's idea of a joke? Had she copied the addresses and put something else inside? With trembling fingers she ripped them open and took out—her own letters. This was a miracle! Her heart filled with incredible joy as she crushed the letters into a ball and flung them in the direction of the waste-paper basket. She went into the kitchen to put on the kettle, singing lustily as she did so.

How lovely it was to be off duty during the day and to have her very own room, where from the window she could see women hanging out their washing and shouting to each other. From the kitchen window, too, she could see a slice of life as lived in the East End. And soon she would be in her beloved Cornwall in a brand new hospital, and she would not feel entirely alone, because Nigel would be there. Life was wonderful!

CHAPTER TEN

As THE weeks passed and the day when the examination results would be out drew nearer everybody concerned became jittery. Girls who had skimped on their studies were now regretting it, as the thought of failure loomed like imminent thunder. Emma was cautiously pleased with the answers she had given, but hesitated from feeling too confident in case she overrated them. Dorothy was unexpectedly reticent over her applications and merely said she had had several acceptances. It was generally known that the results would be published during the third week of the month. Today was the middle of the third week.

Emma was glad they were busy in Casualty, which gave her little time to worry. To have been on Sister Darling's ward knowing she was probably ill-wishing her and would be ready to look pleased if she failed would have been unbearable.

A man who had dropped a crate of tins of soup on his foot had been brought in for X-ray. They showed no bones were broken, but his toes were badly bruised and swollen. Emma had just finsihed bandaging them when a stretcher bearing a small boy whose face was bleeding profusely was carried in. He looked silent and shocked, but his mother was hysterical, repeating in a high querulous voice, 'I'll never get over it, never ever!'

Sister Telford, alerted by the noise, came out of her room to ask the ambulanceman for particulars.

'Name of Hodge, 6 Station Approach—lad savaged by Dobermann. Facial injuries and suffering shock.'

It was difficult to hear what he was saying because of the mother's screaming.

'Thank you, Fred. Take him through to cubicle two, please.' The Sister turned to Emma. 'Will you get on to Dr Shaw and ask him to come down, please. Then see to the mother, who's in shock. Get her some sweetened tea and we'll see what that does for her.'

After putting the call out for Dr Shaw Emma went to the canteen and brought the tea to the mother, who sat in a curtained-off area which was kept for similar occasions. She tried to push the cup away while she endeavoured to peer between the curtains in search of her son.

'Drink some tea, dear, it will make you feel better,' Emma urged gently.

The woman sipped, then gulped, and although she was still distraught she calmed down a little. When she had finished drinking Emma asked if she could tell her waht had happened.

She gave a shuddering sigh. 'My Peter was out the front doin' no harm to nobody, swinging on the gate, although I've told 'im time and again he'll 'ave it off its 'inges, but he didn't take no notice—well, they don't, do they, not unless you clip them round the ear, and that don't seem to make no difference. But this—I'll never get over it, never ever——'

Emma interrupted her before she could start her screaming again. 'And then what happened, Mrs Hodge?'

'That bloomin' dog, he was barkin' 'is head off—he always does, we got rotten neighbours, I'll 'ave the law on them, I will, they'll 'ave to get him destroyed. Bark, bark, bark all the time!'

'How did it manage to attack Peter, then?' Emma raised her voice to be heard.

'Oh, my poor Peter, I didn't know that bloomin' dog was vicious!'

'How did it get out?'

'Well, you know what boys is. Every time the gate 'it the fence this bloomin' dog barks 'is bleedin' 'ead off. Well, Peter—'e's only a boy, all said and done—well, 'e copied 'im—boys do, don't they? This dog went all frantic and threw 'isself like a bleedin' ton weight against the fence—it 'ad been rotten for a long time and it give way, and the next thing I know I 'ears Peter screamin' and screamin' and that dog snarlin' something awful!' Mrs Hodge covered her face with her hands.

Emma waited for a moment, then prompted her gently, 'And then?'

'Then I runs out and there—there was my Peter on the ground and this dog like a great wolf snarlin' and standing over 'im—'is great teeth—I never seen nothin' like it!' The woman covered her face with her hands. She suddenly screamed, 'My God! 'is poor face, what's 'e done to it?'

'What a terrible shock it was for you both. But try not to worry now, because Peter is in good hands. The doctor will be along soon to tell you the extent of his injuries and what they're doing for him. I'd like you to wait here quietly for the time being. All right?'

The woman seemed dazed now and was quiet, so Emma left her to get back to her other patients. Eventually she saw Nigel and hurried across to him, as if she were a homing pigeon.

'Is he going to be all right?'

'I hope so. He's a brave kid. Where's the boy's mother?' he asked.

'She's waiting to hear news of him and is very distressed—naturally. Can you tell her anything yet?'

Nigel tossed his fair hair back off his forehead. 'It was a nasty attack. Lead me to her, will you?'

Emma held the curtain back for him. He sat in the chair beside Mrs Hodge and looked down at her kindly.

'We're keeping Peter in because of shock and we want to keep an eye on him,' he began.

'How is he, Doctor? How's 'is poor face?' She wrung her hands together.

'He's been very fortunate because his eyes are perfectly all right. The wounds are not as severe as I feared, now they've been cleaned and stitched. He looks a bit of a wounded soldier at the moment will all the bandaging, but between you and me he's quite proud of it—it asked for a mirror,' Nigel said with a small laugh. 'I've given him an injection and informed the police. When he leaves hospital he'll need to come back for further injections, but you'll be told about that at the time. I've also given him a sedative to calm him down. Nurse will take you to see him when the Ward Sister gives permission, and I would rather you only stayed for a moment to take a peep at him. I don't want him to be excited.' He gave her a reassuring smile. 'Try not to worry, Mrs Hodge.'

She put out her hand as if to detain him, then withdrew it. 'He—he won't 'ave no scars, will he?'

He avoided looking at her. 'It's impossible to say with any certainty at this stage. There are bound to be scars, but they can fade. If there should be any unsightly scarring which persisted we would consider plastic surgery——'

'Plastic surgery?' she screamed. 'His face is ruined!'

'No, Mrs Hodge, no. Quite possibly there'll be no lasting damage, but if there should be then something can be done about it. Do you understand? Don't worry, Peter's a healthy lad.' He glanced at Emma, gave a reassuring wink and left.

'You wait here, Mrs Hodge, and I'll come for you when we can go up to Peter. All right?'

Emma returned to the other patients. A man and his wife sat staring into space. She noticed that the man's hand had been professionally bandaged and asked them why they were waiting.

The wife replied. 'My husband is waiting to see the Orthopaedic surgeon.'

'The Orthopaedic surgeon? Have you an appointment?'

The woman nudged her husband. 'You got your card?'

He fumbled awkwardly in his pocket and slowly produced it. Emma read it and looked at him in surprise.

'So why are you waiting here?'

'He had his fingers operated on to straighten them, they was all curled up, and he was told to come back today. It says so on his card,' his wife said.

'Yes, I see. But I'm afraid you're in the wrong department. Come with me and I'll show you where to wait. This is the Casualty department, and you want Outpatients.'

When Emma returned she rang the children's ward to enquire whether Peter was ready to see his mother.

'Yes, bring her up. That's Nurse Glover, isn't it?'

'Yes, speaking.'

'I thought I recognised your voice. Did you know the results are out?'

Emma's heart leapt. 'I didn't know. Have you heard any of the results?'

'No, they've just been pinned up on the notice board. Good luck, anyway.'

'Thanks, Jean, same to you.'

Emma hurried across to Mrs Hodge. 'Would you like

to come up now? Please remember what Doctor said and don't excite Peter, that's very important.'

The children's ward was a joy to see, with all the toys and the coloured pictures and the children running around. Mrs Hodge ran forward, shrieking,

'Peter, my baby!'

Emma held her arm firmly. 'Please, Mrs Hodge, calm yourself.'

Sister Frost came towards them and stood authoritatively in front of them.

'You may see your son for one moment only—we want him to rest. If you must speak please lower your voice.' She stalked a few yards away and stood on guard like an avenging angel.

Peter did indeed look like a wounded soldier, with only a small part of his face visible. His eyes seemed blank because of his sedative, but he managed to say hoarsely,

'That bleedin' dog, I 'opes they shoot 'im!'

''Twas your own fault, always teasin' the life out of 'im, you know damn well you are. It serves you right what he done.' Having got that off her chest his mother crooned, 'My poor baby, oh, my poor baby!'

Emma touched her arm. 'I think we'd better go now. You can tell Peter you'll be in to see him to-morrow.'

When she had gone Emma sped up the stairs and along the corridor to the notice board where the results were to be posted. Before she reached it she stood still to regain her breath. Now it hit her, the tremendous importance of what she might read there—or might not. The years of studying, the hopes, the fears; the humiliation she would suffer if she had to admit to her friends and relations that she had failed; the emptiness of the future and the knowledge that she would have to start all over again—not nursing, for if she had failed she would have to recognise the fact that she was not suitable. But she would have to find something. A group of nurses were gathered around the board peering at the list, being patted on the back or given a comforting hug. Emma felt she couldn't join them, she would come back later. She was a coward, she knew she was, but she slunk into the lift and returned to Casualty.

'Good, Nurse, I'm glad to see you back. Did the boy's mother settle down? She had a very nasty shock and I expected to give her a sedative,' Sister Telford said.

'Oh——' Emma knew she should have thought of that. 'Oh, I think she was all right, Sister. She could see that Peter was comfortable, and that was what mattered to her.'

The Sister looked a little anxious. 'I hope so. But remember in future to consult me before allowing somebody to leave when they're so badly shocked. Better safe than sorry.'

'Yes, Sister, I'll remember.'

The next patient had caught her fingers in the machine in the factory where she worked. They were purple, swollen and very painful.

'We'll get it X-rayed for the doctor,' Emma said. 'If you'll come with me, please.'

When the radiographer sent the plates down Emma looked around for a doctor who was free and saw Nigel scrubbing at the sink.

'Dr Shaw, I have a patient with a badly bruised hand, it was caught in some machinery. I've had X-rays done and they're ready if you're free to see them.'

Nigel turned to her with a smile. 'I'll be with you right away. What do the pictures show?'

She shook her head. 'A lot of shadows as far as I'm concerned.'

He held them up against a screen. 'Mm, there's a

fracture of the index and middle fingers.' He pointed them out to Emma.

'How on earth can you read them?' she asked, staring at the blurs.

'With experience,' Nigel replied. 'Hands are of immense importance, and any injury must always be treated with great care. I'll see the patient, and will you tell Rene I'd like her to do the plastering, please.' He smiled. 'She's the best one we have at the job.'

Emma led him to the cubicle where the patient was waiting. As she was going to contact Rene Blake Nigel called her back. 'By the way, the results are out. Did you know?'

Emma flushed as she shook her head. She cursed herself for being so honest that she could never lie convincingly. 'I haven't looked at them yet,' she explained.

She need not have worried, for he was giving all his attention to his patient and didn't even notice her leave.

The row of patients was growing smaller. There was a woman with an abscess under her arm which needed a doctor's attention and a girl with some inflamed scratches on her face.

'What happened?' Emma asked.

'I was looking in a shop window and a cat sprang down on me from the flats above. It landed on my head with its claws out and scratched me as it slithered on down.'

'How awful! Cats are usually more skilful at finding a landing place. Do you live in the flats?'

'Me? Oh no. I work in an office and was looking around the shops in my lunch hour. The boss sent me here, he said you couldn't be too careful.'

'He was quite right. I'll get those scratches cleaned up and the doctor will give you an injection.'

Once again it was Nigel who gave the injection. 'Been up to see the results yet?' he asked Emma.

'No, I haven't had time. And I'm putting off the evil moment,' she said ruefully.

He studied the scratches on the girl's face and nodded his approval of the treatment given. 'Animals are not in our good books today, are they, Nurse? We've had casualties caused by cats and dogs this morning. Is your face painful?' he asked the girl.

'A bit. But I'm just thankful it didn't touch my eyes.'

Nigel nodded. 'Would you like me to give you some pain-killers?'

'Oh no, thank you, I'll be all right.'

'If you need some later on contact your doctor,' Nigel said with a caring smile.

He went off to deal with another patient and the girl left. Emma knew that sooner or later she would have to face up to whatever was on the board, when Sister Telford stopped beside her.

'The results are out, dear, why don't you pop up and see them? Oh, it's your lunch hour anyway.'

'Thank you, Sister. Wish me luck?'

'Of course I do, my dear.'

Emma went slowly up the stairs and looked fearfully along the corridor. A few nurses were standing by the board. She sidled in behind them and with beating heart looked at the list of names. One of the first she saw was BISHOP D. So Dorothy was through. Then she looked for DARK, putting off the evil moment of looking for her own. And yes, Celia was successful too. Her eyes blurred as they skimmed along the list to G. There was GEARING, GOW and GREEN, but no Glover. She ran the tip of her tongue across her dry lips. Oh God, she had failed! She felt numb and empty. The nurses in front of her were apparently successful, because they sounded happy. As they turned to leave they caught sight of Emma.

One of them asked, 'Any luck?'

Emma stared at her bleakly and shook her head.

'Are you sure? Your name is Glover, isn't it?'

'Yes, Emma Glover.'

All the girls studied the list as if the name might be hiding somewhere.

'There it is,' a nurse said, pointing at the board.

Emma leaned forward eagerly. 'No,' she said dejectedly, 'that's CLOVER. It's under the Cs.'

The nurses stared at each other. 'Clover? Do you know anyone of that name? We haven't got a nurse Clover. CLOVER E.—That's a typing error. Hold on a sec.'

The girl ran along the corridor, tapped on a door and afer a few minutes came out again. 'I've just asked to see the register and we haven't got a Clover—I couldn't see one, anyway. It's got to be Glover. That's you, Emma.'

Emma was almost too relieved to feel pleasure, but the awful emptiness had gone.

'Gosh! What a shock it must have been,' said the other nurse. 'We're going along to the local. Coming?'

Most of the successful candidates had gathered there at the inn as this was such a special day. They stood at the bar, and as the others ordered their drinks Emma saw Nigel standing there with a drink in his hand. He caught her eye and smiled and crossed to her, and her heart leapt.

There was a watchful expression on his face as he looked down at her and asked gently, 'Are congratulations in order?'

She gave him a radiant smile. 'Yes, isn't it wonderful? You know, I was devasted because I couldn't see my name there at first. They put it in the wrong column and I nearly had a heart attack. But it turned out they'd made a mistake and put me under the Cs. But apparently my name should have been there.'

He chucked her under the chin affectionately. 'Silly girl, of course it was there. Let me buy you a drink. What are you having?'

Her eyes sparkled. Whatever she had it would taste like champagne.

'A tomato juice, please.'

'Worcester sauce?'

'Please.'

As he passed her the drink he said: 'Congratulations on a well-deserved result.'

She gazed up at him wide-eyed. 'Do you really mean that?'

Nigel raised his eyebrows. 'Of course I do. Haven't you any confidence in your own ability?'

'Recently I've had my doubts,' she said ruefully.'

He shook his head smilingly. 'One word of reproof and you think you're hopeless! You must have faith in yourself, you know. If there were two people and one said you were a good nurse and the other disagreed, you'd believe the latter, wouldn't you?'

Emma nodded thoughtfully. 'Yes, I probably would.'

Just then the barman signalled to him and he apologised to Emma. 'I'm sorry, but it's a call for me,' he said, and touching her arm affectionately, he left to answer it.

No day had ever been made so wonderful. She had

passed her examinations and Nigel had bought her a drink and chatted to her. How lucky she was!

CHAPTER ELEVEN

THERE WAS an end-of-term feeling at supper that evening when Emma, Celia and Dorothy actually sat down together to eat.

'Isn't it smashing all of us have passed? It would have been dreadful if one of us had failed. To tell you the truth, I thought I had, because there was a typing error on the list and my name didn't come under the Gs but Clover E. Can you imagine how I felt?' Emma said with a laugh.

Dorothy looked at her from her heavy-lidded eyes. 'Are you sure about that?'

'Sure? How do you mean?'

'Couldn't it have been Eileen Clover who passed?'

'Eileen Clover?' Emma stared at Dorothy with stricken eyes and felt sick inside. She pushed her plate aside. 'I—I didn't know there was a nurse called Clover.' This was worse than if she had never thought she had passed.

Dorothy raised her eyebrows. 'Didn't you?'

Celia looked at her in disgust. 'Stop it, Dorothy!' She turned to Emma. 'Take no notice, she's having you on, it's her idea of a joke. She knows perfectly well the name has been changed on the board now.'

Emma turned to Dorothy indignantly. 'Is that true?'

Dorothy shrugged and contrived to look innocent.

'But I didn't say anything wrong, I merely asked if it couldn't have been Eileen Clover.'

'You're rotten!' Emma thew a cushion at her, but missed, of course. 'Thank goodness I'll soon be leaving you.'

'Oh yes, you're going to Somerset, aren't you?' Dorothy looked self-satisfied.

'No, I'm not, I'm going to St Joseph's.'

'But you wrote and told them you weren't taking up the vacancy, that's what you said.'

'And so I did.' It was Emma's turn to look pleased. 'But you didn't post my letters, did you?'

For once Dorothy looked taken aback. 'Didn't I? So you've decided to work with Sister Darling again. Be home from home, won't it?'

Emma looked at her triumphantly. 'Your information desk has let you down this time. Sister Darling is not going to St Joseph's, she's staying on here, but on the Administrative side.'

For once Dorothy was silenced. Celia broke the silence.

'You haven't told us where you're going, or haven't you been accepted anywhere?'

Dorothy gave a smug smile. 'I'm not going anywhere. I'm staying on here as a staff nurse.'

'Here? As a staff nurse? But we were told if wasn't worth applying as there were so few vacancies,' Emma said.

'You shouldn't take too much notice of things you're told. I would have thought you'd learned that by now, Emma.'

Emma sighed and still felt shaken from the shock Dorothy had given her. She had suffered so much from her at times that now she felt compelled to say,

'Well, congratulations anyway. You'll still have your flat here and the infinite pleasure of Sister Darling's eagle eye on you even from a distance. Aren't you lucky!'

'Sister Darling won't bother me. Anyhow, she'll be leaving soon.'

Emma opened her mouth to ask what she meant. Could it be anything to do with Nigel? She eyed Dorothy doubtfully. It would probably be wiser not to ask.

When they had cleared away the dishes they sat on the three hard chairs and stared at the television.

'Are you watching this?' Dorothy asked.

It was obvious they weren't. So Dorothy tried all the other channels, but there was nothing which interested them.

'Shall I switch off?'

'Might as well.'

Dorothy went back to her chair and took out her cigarettes. She tried again and again to get her lighter to work, and not for the first time Emma wished that if she had to smoke she would use matches.

Dorothy dragged on her cigarette. 'The next thing is the party.'

'Mm. I wonder what it'll be like.'

'The Auld Lang Syne lark, saying goodbye to everybody who's leaving, pretending you're going to miss them. It's all a farce. Of course, there are doctors who'll be leaving too.'

So of course Nigel would be there. 'I wonder what sort of thing we ought to wear?' Emma asked, forgetting for the moment that Dorothy

Dorothy would more than likely tell her the wrong thing.

But Celia hadn't forgotten. Shooting a scathing glance at Dorothy, she said, 'Just a pretty dress, Emma. But haven't you been to any of the other parties when people have left?'

Emma shook her head. 'No, they always seemed to be held when I was away. Do you think they were trying to tell me something?' Her thoughts went to her practically empty wardrobe. 'I haven't really got anything suitable here, but it would be simpler to buy something than bother to get Mum to send one up.'

'We could go on a shopping spree,' Dorothy suggested, but Emma decided she would prefer to go alone.

On her next afternoon off she took the Underground to Oxford Circus and browsed around the stores. The dresses hanging on racks seemed drab and uninteresting and she had a great urge to buy something really outstanding, just—just to please herself. It had nothing to do with the fact that Nigel would be at the party, because that would be silly. As she sat in the tea-room of one of the stores with a toasted tea-cake and a pot of tea she closed her eyes and let herself dream of wearing a model gown and being escorted by a well-dressed man who looked down at her with warmth and admiration. When she looked up at him she saw his eyes were amber and green-flecked, and she gave an exclamation of annoyance with took her out of her dream and back to the more likely present, with her wearing one of those drab dresses and sitting alone. Well, she would probably be alone, but she was hanged if she was going to buy one of those dresses.

She paid her bill, then decided to try the roads leading off Oxford Street. Here there was a more interesting selection, or else the dresses looked better because there were fewer of them. On a model in one of the windows was a green and white patterned dress with a peplum. The shaped belt, collar and cuffs on the short sleeves were green satin, and Emma decided it was the dress for her. Unfortunately it wasn't priced, but she asked to try it on. It fitted like a dream, the peplum accentuated her small waist. It didn't cost more than she had expected to pay, and as this was a present to herself for passing her exams she bought it. On her way out of the store she saw some green ribbon in exactly the same shade, so she bought a length, not knowing just what she would do with it.

In the evening Emma had letters to write, one to St Joseph's telling them she had passed her exams and looked forward to taking up the appointment with them on the third of the month as arranged. She also told them she would be requiring hostel accommodation. She had thought about that for a long time, because the hospital was not far from her home and she would have liked to live there with Wendy and her parents, but the bus service was not geared to the hours she would be expected to work and she would be unable to go home when she only had a short time off duty. One day, maybe, she would buy a car. At the thought she was reminded of Derek and his never-ending ambitions, and she laughed.

The days were creeping by, and Casualty was not holding her attention as it had previously. She believed agency nurses might feel like this; the patients' welfare was as important as ever, but you did not feel a part of it all because you would be moving on.

On the day of the party Emma felt as excited as she had when she was a child, when parties were of vital importance and not to be invited to one was only

marginally better than death. People who apparently
did not know of this imminent celebration came off the
streets with sprains and cuts as if it was an ordinary day.
The hours were passing slowly. Then in the afternoon a
group of men and women who had been to a luncheon
party in a nearby hotel came in vomiting and with
stomach pains suffering from food poisoning. Some
patients were obviously more severely affected than
others, and doctors were sent for and wards alerted in
case there would be admissions.

While Emma was attending to the patients she was
aware of the comforting presence of Nigel, for she felt
that if he was there everything would be all right. One
woman who had a history of a gastric ulcer had to be
admitted; another who was in her late seventies was to
be kept in, at least overnight, and Emma had to ring
Sister Darling to tell her they were being sent to her
ward. Apparently she did not recognise Emma's
voice, because she could hardly have been helpful or
pleasant.

'Thank you, Nurse, I'll get the beds prepared.
And will you tell the doctor I can make room for—
let me see—five—no, four more patients if re-
quired.'

Only one man was severely affected, and he was
reluctant to be admitted, saying between groans that his
wife was pregnant and he didn't want her to be alone so
near her time. But Nigel was adamant.

'You wouldn't be much use to her in this state. We'll
let her know that you're here and there's nothing for her
to worry about.'

'But if she should start during the night—I must get
back!'

'If that were to happen she'd ring her doctor or, if
necessary, an ambulance. I'm sure she'll be perfectly all

right.'

Emma listened with interest. At one time she might have thought Nigel was uncaring, but not now. He was being sensible and calm because it was best for everybody concerned. Her heart swelled with admiration and love.

It was late when Emma went off duty, but at least the party casualties had all been dealt with. The bus was crowded and smelly, and the thought of the car she might one day have loomed tantalisingly in her mind.

She went thankfully into the flat. She could hear Dorothy splashing around in the bath, so she put on the kettle for tea. She took a cup into the living room, kicked off her shoes and sprawled in the uncomfortable chair. Tomorrow she would have to pack her belongings and remember to say goodbye to anyone whom she didn't see tonight. In a strange sort of way she was going to miss Dorothy more than Celia. Dorothy, partly because of her size but mostly because of her personality, was someone she would always remember, even though it might not be with affection, whereas Celia was a shadowy character who would never stay in her mind.

Dorothy came out of the bathroom pink and damp wearing a blue housecoat with a torn hem.

'Hi! Any tea in the pot?'

Emma lifted the lid and nodded. 'Enough for a little one.'

'I hope you're referring to me and not the cup.'

'You? A little one? That'll be the day! What are you going to wear?'

'I thought maybe my silver lamé, the Bruce Oldfield one, it always looks nice.'

'Emma's eyes widened. 'Bruce Oldfield? How long have you had that?'

Dorothy sighed. 'Don't be daft! I'll wear my blue from C&A—it's the only one I've got isn't it?'

'Tough luck. I'll have my bath now, we haven't too much time. Do you know if Celia's going?'

Dorothy rolled her eyes heavenwards. 'What? Celia go to a den of iniquity? You must be joking!'

Emma mopped up the water that Dorothy had spilled everywhere and decided a shower would be more invigorating than a bath. When she had towelled herself dry she went into her room to get ready. Taking her new dress from the wardrobe, she laid it on the bed and thought how pretty it looked. Would it look just as good on her? She slipped it over her head with a feeling of apprehension. Say she'd put on weight since she bought it? There was the steak and kidney pudding she had had for dinner the other day and—oh yes—a chocolate bar. She held her breath and pulled in her stomach muscles until she had fastened it, then breathed a sigh of relief. It fitted like a dream. She stood away from the mirror to see that the length was right, then twisted around to get a view of the back. She was very satisfied. Now what to do with her hair. Pinned she felt like a woman in a girl's dress; hanging loose made her feel all head, so she plaited it and half way down tied it with the green ribbon. When she had put on a little eye-shadow and some lipstick she was quite pleased with her appearance. She took the wickedly expensive perfume she had bought and seldom used from her drawer and sprayed it on her neck and arms, hoping whoever came close would appreciate the heavenly scent. They jolly well ought to, they'd be smelling it for free.

It was time they were leaving, so she put on her coat, picked up her handbag and called to Dorothy.

'Are you ready yet?'

'Coming.' Dorothy emerged from her bedroom with

the inevitable cigarette dangling from her mouth, a cascade of ash down the front of her tightly fitting royal blue satin dress.

'That's a lovely colour for you, Dorothy, it brings out the colour of your eyes,' Emma said generously.

'Thanks. Undo you coat, then, and let me see yours.'

Emma did so reluctantly, vowing not to mind when Dorothy said something disparaging. But she didn't.

'It's really nice,' she said. Emma scoffed at herself, for she felt a sudden surge of pleasure on hearing the words.

Outpatients had been cleared for the party and some enthusiasts had pinned up a few balloons and streamers. Mike Heller, a porter who had once been a holiday camp red-coat, was in charge. He started the music, too loudly at first, then toned it down before crossing to the buffet to cast an eye over the food and check there were bottle openers and enough glasses. Then he went into the kitchen where Nurse Smithers and Staff Nurse Williams were setting out cups and saucers and preparing the tea and coffee urn.

'Have you got enough spoons, girls?' he asked.

'You're out of touch, Mike, not many well-trained staff take sugar, you know.'

He winked. 'Then they're not like me. Three spoonfuls is my choice. Couldn't drink it without.'

Everyone seemed to arrive at once and soon the room was filled with nurses only vaguely familiar in their party dresses. Keeping to their own side of the room were the doctors and consultants and their wives. There seemed a generation gap between both groups, the older men in dark suits with neatly brushed hair, or balding, and the younger ones in casual clothes and with longer hair. The wives, too, were different from the

nurses. Whereas the nurses wore brightly coloured
dresses—some even wore mini-skirts—the doctors'
wives were dressed discreetly in muted colours and their
hair was smooth and neatly groomed. A group of
medical students who Emma rightly guessed had been
urged to put in an appearance to boost the number of
men stood around looking anywhere but at the nurses.
Emma wondered what the programme was going to be;
nobody seemed to know. She saw a few people with
drinks in their hands, so she went across to where a
young man, unknown to her, was dispensing them.
Dorothy had disappeared from her side and was now at
the far side of the room with Heather, the nurse with
whom she had been hoping to go on holiday.

Emma took her drink and sat on a chair by the wall to
watch what the others were doing. The doctors' wives
didn't seem too happy, and Emma sympathised. They
probably didn't know one another, whereas the doctors
were colleagues and chatted amongst themselves. But all
the time Emma was watching the door to see when Nigel
would arrive.

Then, with a sudden thrill which vanished as quickly
as it arrived, she saw him. He had on a dark suit. She
had never seen him dressed like that before, and in
contrast his hair looked fairer. His head was bent—and
then she saw why. He was looking down at Sister
Darling, who accompanied him. She had cleverly
contrived to look neither like the wives nor the nurses
but something in between. She wore a dress not unlike's
Emma's, only black and white and a little longer.
Around her neck she wore a string of pearls to match
her stud earrings. There was no stupid, girlish pigtail for
her, instead her beautifully layered fair hair stood away
from her forehead and behind her ears. Emma
grudgingly admitted to herself that she looked really
outstanding. She wondered gloomily why she had gone
to the expense of buying this dress. She might have

known she couldn't compete with Sister Darling, who had everything, including Nigel. As far as Emma was concerned she could keep everything she got if only she would keep her hands off him. She sipped her drink thoughtfully. Even if she did what difference would it make to her? She had to face it, Nigel never had been and never would be in the least interested in her. He had given her a lift a couple of times and spoken to her, whereas doctors usually ignored student nurses. On the other hand, he had told her off many, many times. So why on earth was she so stupid as to think about him so much? They stood with a group of doctors, and Sister Darling seemed to have as much to say as Nigel, and of course she would, because she knew them all. She had the edge on the other wives and on the nursing staff. She would make him an admirable wife, and the fact that she had a nasty nature would not matter at all because he could be nasty too. Yes, Emma sighed, they were right for each other.

There are nothing for her here, so she would get something to eat and then go home. She did not like parties. As she was filling her plate at the buffet she saw Nigel doing the same, only he had two plates on a tray. He reached across to the chicken vol-au-vents and jerked her arm by mistake.

'So sorry,' he said. Then seeing it was Emma he smiled. 'Hello. having a good time?'

'Not particularly. There isn't a lot to do, is there?'

He glanced around at the few couples who were talking together.

'I suppose not. Have you heard where you'll be moving to?'

She looked at him defiantly. 'To St Joseph's,' she said.

She supposed he was using his bedside manner, because he looked pleased. 'Then we'll be together again.' He looked doubtfully at the sausage rolls, then asked as if the thought had just struck him. 'When are you travelling down?'

Emma was suddenly filled with hope. 'Tomorrow night,' she said, looking up at him.

He thought better of the sausage rolls and chose wholemeal sandwiches. 'Then you'll be down there before me. I don't go until next week.'

She wanted to say, 'I don't need to go tomorrow, I'll wait,' but Nigel studied the plates, and said 'That should be enough,' and seemed to have forgotten she was there.

The food tasted as if it had come from the canteen, and it probably had. A couple of nurses who she knew slightly sat on the vacant chairs beside her. They said, 'Hello', and asked where she was going next, and then there was little else to say. Ian Ford, a young houseman whom Emma had occasionally worked with in Casualty, asked her to dance as if he had been told to do so, which was probably the case. By the number of times he trod on her toes she had the feeling he had never been on a dance floor. As they stumbled across the room she heard a sniffing and looked up swiftly. He wasn't crying, was he? Because *she* was the one who was suffering.

He gave an outsize sniff. 'What's that smell?'

'Do you like it?' Emma smiled.

He sniffed again. 'It's—um—whatever is it?'

Emma was about to name her extravagance when he gave a triumphant exclamation.

'I've got it—it's air-freshener, the stuff they put in the loo. I knew I recognised it!''

Just then they stumbled again, and this time Emma made certain hers was the foot on top. See how he liked it!

Mike Heller stopped the music and called for silence.

'I think they're going to announce Dr Shaw's engagement to Darling,' Ian whispered.

Emma felt as if she had been thumped in the stomach. Mike continued talking, but Emma could not hear what he said because of the buzzing in her ears. Then Dr Cotleigh, the senior consultant, stood up. He wished everybody who was leaving the best of luck in the future and told them they should always remember they were Nightingale trained and to live up to its excellent reputation. His speech was short and he looked tired. Emma had no doubt he and his silver-haired wife would be leaving in the next few minutes.

'I'm working tonight, so I'll push off now,' Ian said.

Emma stood for a moment wondering why she had come here and eager now to go home. She caught sight of Dorothy and went across to her.

'I'm going now. How about you?'

'Yes, I'm coming. Strictly speaking I shouldn't be here, it's a party for those who are leaving.'

'Where's Heather going?'

Dorothy shook her head. 'She didn't pass. She did too much agency work, I suppose.'

'What a shame. So what's she going to do?'

'Stay on and take them again. But she won't do agency work. That's what she says now, but it'll be a different story later on.'

Outside the building Emma turned to look at it. It was huge and shabby, had been standing there for years. She had been happy there and sad. But despite all the ups and downs she would be sorry to leave.

CHAPTER TWELVE

EMMA HAD said goodbye to the hospital and later to Celia. Now it left only Dorothy and the flat. Celia had already gone to join her boyfriend in Nottingham prior to going to Malawi, but was cagey as to whether or not they would be getting married before leaving England.

For once Emma felt sorry for Dorothy. Most of the other students had the excitement of moving on, but although strictly speaking she had done better than any of them in being apppointed to Nightingale's, it seemed somehow an anti-climax to carry on here as if nothing had happened.

When Emma was ready to leave, Dorothy, who was smoking and staring into space, said unexpectedly,

'Do you mind if I come to Paddington with you?'

Emma looked at her in surprise. 'Of course not. But what will you do when you get there?'

Dorothy shrugged her heavy shoulders. 'Come back, of course. But it'll be something to do.'

Emma felt a rush of sympathy. 'I'd like you to come, but the taxi will be here any minute. Are you ready?'

Dorothy nodded, lumbered into her room and emerged almost immediately wearing her coat and outdoor shoes. That was a good thing about Dorothy, she was always on time. No doubt that was one reason why she had been kept on at Nightingale's.

There was a ring at the door and Emma took a last look around the drab room. The clock on the mantlepiece had stopped again; nobody ever thought it was their job to wind it. Crushed paper and cigarette stubs still lay on the floor around the waste-paper basket. The room would be greatly improved with a few coloured cushions and ornaments if someone ever got around to buying them. It had been good having her own bedroom. She picked up her suitcase.

'I wonder who'll move in here—have you heard?'

'No. I'm hoping it'll be Heather. Better go.'

Emma smiled to herself as Susan Clay's door creaked open. She just had to see that long nose again.

'I'm off, Mrs Clay!' she called out.

But the door closed softly. The nose would have to be a memory.

In the taxi Emma looked eagerly from side to side at the shabby streets as if she liked them and didn't want to leave. The truth was she was used to them and they did not seem so sinister now. She wondered if she would ever come this way again, but doubted it. Once back in Cornwall she would have no need to come to London. If she wanted large stores or a theatre there was Plymouth only half the distance away.

Dorothy was quiet and seemed lost in thought, and Emma realised that she knew nothing of her background and now she never would. Then they were at Paddington, making their way to the busy departure platform. It gave Emma a feeling of excitement tempered by one of sadness as she saw Dorothy standing large and silent and going nowhere.

She shook her hand impulsively. 'I'll miss you,' she said.

Dorothy nodded. 'Keep in touch, kid.'

Emma felt embarrassed and was relieved to hear the doors slamming and then the momentary hush before the train began sliding out of the station.

'Good luck!' she called from the window.

Dorothy raised her hand and stood watching until Emma could no longer see her.

Because of the expense of hiring the taxi Emma had decided to make do without a sleeper and to doze in her corner seat. By the time the journey had come to an end she doubted the wisdom of her action. She had had a series of short naps which had left her with a stiff neck and heavy eyes.

She was glad to see her father waiting at the station exit.

'You're a darling,' she grinned, then added cheekily, 'Couldn't you sleep?'

He shot her a look. 'D'you want to walk home?'

'Are the others still in bed?'

'I expect Wendy is, but your mother's up. To tell the truth, she woke me up with a cup of tea or I might not have been here.'

After the narrow streets she had left, Penzance promenade looked wide and newly washed. Emma opened her window and leaned out to breathe the salty air and feast her eyes on the expanse of rippling sea. She was surprised that flags had not been put on to herald her arrival, for indoors the table was laid out lavishly and there was a delicious smell of bacon frying.

'Hello, Mum, how are you? This is luxury indeed. To have such a breakfast and to be waited on too!'

'Well, this is a special occasion. It's grand to know you'll be working nearby and not hundreds of miles away.'

When breakfast was over Emma took her mother's advice and went to bed. As she laid her head on the pillow she could still seem to feel the movement of the train and see the passing scene and felt certain she would not sleep. But when she awoke it was lunchtime. In the afternoon she went to the shops with Wendy.

'What are you going to do now you've left school?' she asked her sister.

Wendy wrinkled her nose. 'I'm going as an apprentice hairdresser with Philippe in Causewayhead. I don't know that I fancy being stuck amongst all that hair and water, though.'

'You mustn't think of that side of it. I mean, if you think of Casualty you think you'd hate to be amongst all that blood and vomit, but it's different when you're actually working there. You're interested in what you're doing and seeing their nice clean bandages when they leave. I should think it was like that in hairdressing. They come in with their hair looking a mess and you get your pleasure in making it look nice. It should be very satisfying.'

Wendy appeared to brighten up. 'D'you ever see anything of that dishy doctor, the one who brought you down last time?'

'Yes, I saw him all the time in Casualty—well, most of the time.'

'I suppose you won't see him any more now.'

'Yes, I will,' Emma said happily. 'He's going to St Joseph's too.'

Wendy's eyes shone. 'Is that because you're going there?'

Emma puffed out her cheeks. 'Heavens, no! He'd arranged to go there ages before I did.'

'So is that why you're going there?'

Emma stood still. 'I'm going there because it's near home and I love Cornwall. But I'm beginning to dislike the people. You're as bad as Mum at trying to make something of Dr Shaw giving me a lift down here. Once and for all, he's engaged to a beastly Sister at Nightingale's. And even if he wasn't it wouldn't make a scrap of difference—doctors aren't interested in student nurses.'

'But you're not a student nurse now, you're staff, aren't you?' Wendy said mischeviously.

'Have you seen Derek lately?' Emma was determined to change the subject.

Wendy laughed. 'He's a pain, him and his ruddy car. Honestly, he makes us curl up the way, he gets himself all togged up in that ridiculous cap, long scarf and all.

And when he isn't driving around where he thinks everyone he knows will see him he's polishing the damn thing with his mother's red knickers.'

'With his *what*?' Emma spluttered.

'It's true. He happened to drop them when Sandra was passing and she could hardly tell us for laughing. She said 'Oops, Derek, you've dropped your knickers,' but he didn't cotton on.'

'You're a mean lot! I thought you liked Derek.'

'Well, I did, but that car has changed him. He's daft about it.'

Emma pictured Derek's prim and proper mother, who never appeared in public without a hat and gloves, and seemd very strait-laced.

'I can't see his mother wearing red knickers,' she said thoughtfully.

'Not now you can't. Derek's using them to polish his——

Emma punched her sister and they walked on, laughing.

On Sunday afternoon Mr Glover drove Emma to the hospital so that she could get settled in before starting work the next day.

Nigel had not exaggerated, it was indeed well-equipped, with sparkling tiles and gleaming chromium, and Emma's bedsitting-room and microscopic kitchen were charming. There was grey wall-to-wall carpeting, coral curtains and cushions and duvet cover, even the china in the cabinet had a decorative border in coral. This was the prettiest room Emma had ever had, and it had obviously never been used before.

In the evening she went to the canteen—she must remember to refer to it as the Refectory, since that was on the door. There was a feeling of anti-climax when she discovered that the food was no different from that at Nightingale's. Hospital food, she was convinced, came from a source all its own. Quite plainly the room was

used by the entire hospital staff, but Emma didn't mind
betting doctors nurses and porters would all keep to
their own corners. She bought a cup of tea and a
doughnut, then went for a walk over the downs, which
were deserted, the only sounds the movement of the sea
and the cries of the seagulls. This was another world
from the one she had left three hundred miles away.

There was a notice to the effect that she would be
working on Men's Medical Ward. As staff nurse! It was
with trepidation that she went on duty the next day.
Sister Borlase was in charge, and Emma kept her fingers
crossed that she would not be another Sister Darling.
She bore no physical resemblance to her, she was small,
thin and middle-aged.

When Emma introduced herself she smiled in a
pleasant, businesslike manner and immediately got
down to giving her the details of the patients. The men
looked incredibly healthy and wholesome, with swarthy
complexions despite possible temporary pallor, and
were mostly of stocky build. In the main they were
fishermen or farmers suffering from occupational
troubles, and Emma felt she knew and liked them all.
They were people she understood.

Nurse Matthews, who was in her second year, told
Emma she had moved there from Truro hospital to
complete her training.

'I wish they'd sent me to a town somewhere instead of
this god-forsaken hole,' she grumbled.

Emma looked at her in amazement. 'Honestly,
Karen, you don't know what you're saying! It's sheer
bliss being here instead of London.'

'London? You were in London and you came down
here? But there's nothing here.' Karen frowned in
disbelief.

'Perhaps you don't know Cornwall very well. You'll
get to love it in time.'

'Don't know it?' Karen squealed. 'I was born down

here and went to school here, and I'm just dying to get away.'

'And what do you think you'd have in London that you haven't got here?' Emma was keen to hear.

'Everything. Shops, markets, people, theatres, museums, Underground trains——'

Emma nodded. 'True, there is all that. But down here you've got the sea and the scenery and people and things you know and understand. And there's something about Cornwall——'

Karen sniffed. 'Depends what you want, I suppose. Hush! Here comes my heart throb.'

Sister Borlase was accompanying a doctor into the ward. She introduced him to Emma as Dr Worthing. Emma took a good look at him. So he was Karen's pin-up! He was not unattractive, but his fair hair was curly and stood up and away from his forehead, and his eyes were just plain brown and had no colour flecks in them. Karen would see the difference when Nigel arrived. As for herself, Dr Worthing would never cause her heart to beat quicker, and it seemed hard to imagine anyone would feel otherwise. She glanced from him to Karen and saw the colour had risen in the girl's cheeks. He never gave her a second glance until he said sharply.

'You're writing is deplorable and quite indecipherable, Nurse. I know the medical profession is noted for its illegible handwriting, but I urge you to improve yours if you wish to join it.'

When he had gone Karen closed her eyes and said blissfully,

'He spoke to me!'

'Spoke to you? He told you off.'

'To be told off by him is magic. I would happily let him walk over me in hobnailed boots.'

'You'd what?' Emma demanded. 'I'd be furious if anyone spoke to me like that.'

'Then you've never been in love,' Karen said

dreamily, and Emma felt sickened.

But the thought sneaked into her mind that although it sounded awful and degrading there was something inside her that knew what Karen was saying. It was something she herself would have to fight.

She was counting the days until Nigel's arrival and she had to admit there was not a lot of difference in her behaviour and Karen's. It was the same old, old story, silly young nurses falling in love with doctors. It was something, she supposed, to bring a little light and shade into their mundane lives, and there was no harm in that provided they did not take it seriously. And she didn't. Because she knew Nigel and Sister Darling were intended for each other, and if she ever thought of him as anything other than someone else's fiancé she was creating unhappiness for herself and had only herself to blame.

When Emma had ticked off sufficient days in her diary it was as if Christmas had arrived, and she looked out eagerly at the car park. And yes, Nigel's car was there. Perhaps she would see him in the Refectory.

In fact he came into the ward with Dr Worthing and Sister Borlase. Emma's heart leapt with admiration and pride. Compared with him Dr Worthing looked as if he had a perm, and there was nothing outstanding about his appearance. Emma stole a glance at Karen to see what impression he made on her, but the silly girl seemed only to have eyes for Dr Worthing.

As he drew nearer Emma smiled a welcome to Nigel, but he was talking to Dr Worthing and barely nodded back. She tried again when he had finished talking, but this time his attention was entirely on a patient, and she felt snubbed and bitterly disappointed.

When they had gone Karen said, 'That new doctor is quite nice too, isn't he?'

Emma shrugged. 'D'you think so? He's not bad, I suppose, if you like that type. He obviously thinks a lot of himself. But don't they all?' she said miserably.

Emma saw him in the Refectory and several times on the ward during the next week, but on only one occasion did he acknowledge her with a smile, and she nearly missed that because she was turning unhappily away.

Unbelievably she wished she was back at Nightingale's because he had been friendly to her there. Now there was nothing to look forward to, no excitement. She even missed Dorothy.

CHAPTER THIRTEEN

ON THIS sunny afternoon Men's Medical looked deserted and was uncanninly quiet. One by one the patients had shuffled to the adjoining TV room to watch a cricket match, Emma was seated at the centre table in the ward doing her paperwork.

As she filled in the patients' charts her mind wandered. She was surprised not to have heard from Derek and hoped he had not met with an accident in his car. She guessed he would be more upset at scraping his TR7 than in being injured himself. When she was in London the thought of Cornwall had meant the cliffs and the sea and the countryside, forgetting that working in Cornwall would mean being in a hospital ward which could be anywhere.

She closed her eyes for a moment and pictured the north coast with the heather-strewn downs, the sheer cliffs and the aquamarine sea. She heard footsteps and glanced up. Her heart did a somersault, for Nigel was there beside her.

'Sleeping on duty, Staff?' he asked softly.

Her eyes smouldered with anger, but as they met his she saw a hint of a smile in them which filled her with warmth and weakness.

She bit back the sharp reply which had been on her lips. 'No Doctor just picturing for a brief moment the beauty of Cornwall outside the hospital. How can I help you?'

'Mr Penrose. I've no need to ask where he is, I suppose?'

Emma smiled. 'Shall I fetch him for you?'

'And take him away from the match? No, it'll keep.'

She looked at him questioningly. 'Is it bad news, then?'

'It depends on how he looks at it. As you know, his ulcer is not responding to medication, so it's best to get rid of it. He's to be moved to surgical.'

'Oh dear, I can't imagine that will please him.'

Nigel grinned. 'No? Then I'll leave you to tell him. OK?'

'Coward,' Emma said with a sideways smile.

His thick lashes almost hid his eyes, revealing just a hint of green and gold. 'So you think I'm a coward? Then I'd better do something about it. How about going to your Wishing Well and having a shot at wishing I were different? Would it work, do you think?'

'Not now you've told me,' she laughed.

'Will you take me there all the same? Maybe it will work, and I can wish for something else to be on the safe side.'

Emma's breath came fast. Did he mean it, or was he joking? If she said she would take him there would he chuckle and walk away and so make her feel embarrassed to the core? Yet if she ignored his request would he think she didn't want to go there with him?

She hesitated, then replied lightly with a laugh. 'If you believe in magic I'll take you.'

'OK, that's a deal. When are you off duty? Tomorrow?'

She was, and had been intending to go home, but she had promised herself if Nigel ever asked her again to take him there nothing and nobody would stop her.

'Yes, it's my day off.' She looked anxiously towards the ward doors, praying that no one would come in to disturb them.

'Good. Would eleven o'clock suit you?'

Emma nodded. 'Yes.'

'In the car park, then.' He turned to walk away, then turned back. 'Remember to get Mr Penrose moved to Surgical.'

Then he was gone, and she was unbelievably happy. Tomorrow! She crossed to the window and looked up at the sky. It was blue now, but was it too good to last? Would it rain and the outing have to be put off again? How long would they be together? They could get to Madron, visit the Well, make a wish and be back in under an hour. Could she take him on a longer route, or would he know what she was doing and give that knowing smile that made her both love and hate him? What should she wear? When the outing was over where would he leave her because she was not on duty again until Monday morning? So many questions jostled for attention in her mind they were spoiling her pleasure in the moment, so she quashed them and concentrated instead on the time they *would* be together.

With a jolt she realised she had temporarily forgotten Mr Penrose. She was about to go to him when she paused. Another couple of hours would make no difference, so let him be happy as he was.

She woke early the next morning and slipped eagerly from under her duvet to pad across the room to the window. Almost afraid to do so, she parted the curtains and looked out anxiously. The sun was rising, a huge golden disc in a red-streaked sky, and she smiled happily. Although it was early it was pointless going back to bed, because she was wide awake and eager to get started.

She was able to spend longer than usual having a shower and came out fresh and glowing. She sat on the edge of her bed in her towelling robe as she wondered what to wear. Bearing in mind the overgrown area around the Well, she decided on dark green slacks with a lighter shade of green top which would be cool if the day turned hot and warm it stayed cool. She stood in front of the mirror and tried her hair in different ways—as if it were a bun, pulled back in plait or hanging loose, and decided at last because— well, because she knew her hair was her best feature and Nigel had never seen it just hanging. But most of all it was the way she wanted it and nothing to do with him.

Instead of going to the Refectory for breakfast she decided to make tea and toast in her own little kitchen and make it last as long as she could. At last the time had come, and despite the silly young housemen at the party she took out her perfume, sniffed it appreciatively, then sprayed it liberally on herself. She had a moment of doubt. Had she used too much? Nothing worse than reeking of perfume on a lovely morning in the country. She took her face flannel and held it under the tap and tried to wash some of it off, then realised with a start that it was eleven o'clock, so grabbing her handbag, she locked her door and sped out of the hostel and across the lawn (strictly forbidden) and arrived breathlessly in the car park. Nigel was already there cleaning his windscreen, and Emma giggled to herself as she wondered if he was using his mother's knickers.

'Hi,' she said, pausing before she reached him to note how smart he looked in a cream open-necked shirt with rolled-up sleeves and brown slacks.

He glanced up momentarily, then continued what he was doing before looking at her again, and this time she could have sworn there was admiration in his eyes.

'Hello to you,' he said, and tossed his polishing cloth in the back of the car.

Emma eyed it with interest. Was it? It could be. It wasn't an ordinary duster, it——

Nigel watched her intently. 'Are you condemning me for being untidy?'

'Untidy?'

'For throwing my cloth in the back seat instead of putting it away.'

'Oh no. I—um——'

He laughed. 'OK, in you get.'

'Have you got your bent pin?' she asked as he was sliding in beside her.

'Bent pin?'

'Yes, you'll need one to wish with. Remember?'

He shook his head. 'Where would I get a bent pin?'

'Not to worry, I've brought some myself.'

They glided from the hospital grounds on to the main road, which was practically deserted.

'Very different from Brixton, isn't it?' Nigel said.

I'll say. D'you like it down here?'

'What I've seen of it, but I've been pretty busy getting my bearings in the hospital. I shouldn't really be playing truant this morning.'

Emma felt a pang of disappointment. This morning. That sounded as if he would be going straight back as soon as they'd visited Madron.

The moors were breathtakingly beautiful, the carpet of purple heathers and golden gorse seeming to stretch for ever.

'It was at Madron that the news of the victory of the Battle of Trafalgar was first heard,' Emma told him with proprietorial pride.

Nigel raised his eyebrows. 'Quite a place, Madron, and I'd never heard of it before. Mind you, I shouldn't be surprised if other towns and villages had that same boast.'

'Well, anyhow, you should look in the church where there are all kinds of interesting things. There's a brass picture showing a one-time mayor of Penzance with his wife, both in Shakespearean dress. She's got a hooped skirt and a wide-brimmed hat, and their six children are kneeling around them.'

'That was a small family in those days. It's different now, but unfortunately I have a patient with six children who's pregnant again.

'Unfortunately? But that's nothing to worry about, is it?'

'It wouldn't be if she didn't have TB.'

'Oh dear. Would—would she consider having an abortion?'

He shook his head. 'They're Catholics. And that poor lady quite definitely should not be pregnant. Apparently her husband was warned of the danger, but——'

'TB is comparitively rare nowadays, isn't it?'

'Unfortunately not quite so rare in the heart of the country. Quite possibly they drink milk from infected cows.'

'I thought all cows were tested?'

'They're supposed to be. I don't know, there could be other reasons.'

Emma did not want to be talking of work today, but on the other hand she might irritate Nigel if she chatted about Cornish history when his mind was on other things. So she remained silent and enjoyed being with him on this lovely morning in beautiful surrounding. It was something she would always remember.

This was the best time of the year to visit Madron, when the church was surrounded with great bushes of mauve and pink hydrangeas and looked out over the sapphire sea to the pyramid of green foliage which was St Michael's Mount.

Nigel gazed at it for a moment in silence. 'It's almost too beautiful. I'd like to take a picture of that. Will you stand over by the gate?'

'Me? Wouldn't you rather take on just as it is?'

'No.'

Emma stood beside the lychgate feeling self-conscious. He surveyed the scene for a moment, then walked across and placing his hands on her shoulders turned her side-on. At his touch a tremor shot through her arms and set her nerves tingling. Then he ran his firm hands through her hair and arranged it over her shoulder. Their faces were only inches apart, and she made the mistake of raising her eyes and found she was looking straight into his. For a moment their eyes locked, and the strange sensation in her body was something she had never before experienced, something magical which made her long desperately to be held close, to feel Nigel's lips on hers. Surely he felt that too? She could scarcely breathe, and she was afraid to move and so end this wonderful moment. Without being able to stop herself she felt a shiver swept through her. Nigel gave her a knowing look, ran his hand lightly over her hair and said casually,

'Lovely colour. Now can you hold that position?'

He stepped back to take the picture, and she felt as wobbly as a jelly and hoped it wouldn't show in the photograph.

'Shall I take one of you now?' she asked.

He shook his head. 'No thanks. Now that we're here we might as well take a quick look inside.'

Emma heard the sudden muted sound of organ music. 'Oh, we can't—what a pity. There's a service on. But there's a nice thing I'd like you to see in the graveyard.' It was the copper figure of a blindfold girl sitting on a large granite sphere holding a lyre with two broken strings. 'She's green with age and the weather, but I think she looks nicer for that.'

They stopped beside it to read,

A broken string, and through the drift
Of aeons sad with human cries
She waits the Hand of God to lift
The bandage from her eyes.

'It makes you wonder who wrote that and when, and what relationship they had. Was it a parent, a lover or a husband?'

'Maybe it was just a quotation.'

'That's not nearly such a romantic thought,' Emma protested laughingly.

'I must come here again some time, but now we'd better get on.'

When they got back to the car Nigel picked up his camera. 'This should be ready now,' he said, unpeeling the photograph. He looked at it critically. 'I'm afraid it isn't very good.' He handed it to Emma.

'What a shame! All those lovely flowers and I ruin it. I look like an outsize weed in amongst them.'

He gave her a quick glance. 'I think the trouble is the flowers are very colourful and so are you, and you don't need each other. It looks a bit of a mess. However, let's press on. How far is it to the Well?'

'Only a mile or so. Actually, it was a baptistry, but the roof has disappeared. It's a holy well and once upon a time it was as famous as Lourdes.'

'What with wishes coming true and ills being cured all by magic we've got it made. I take it if you live in Cornwall you live happily and healthily for evermore. Tough on the undertakers,' Nigel smiled.

'And on doctors,' she grinned. 'I think you'd better stop somewhere near here, because we'll have to walk the next bit.' She gave him a sideways glance. 'Don't worry, it isn't far.'

They made their way through knee-high nettles and

weeds until they came to the roofless baptistery, its walls covered with ferns and lichen and with an ancient seat and altar hewn from stone still standing. Almost hidden by reeds and grasses was the Well.

'And here,' Emma said grandly as if bestowing a prize, 'Is a bent pin. Stand with your back to the Well, throw the pin over your left shoulder and wish. Be sure you don't say what you're wishing for. Right?'

She had to giggle when she saw him standing there, a large, upright figure, the sun making his hair gleam like gold, taking part in this childish game. She wondered what Sister Darling would think if she could see him!

He turned quickly to see where his pin had fallen.

'I can't see it,' he said, peering in the murky water against the weeds.

Emma laughed unkindly. 'Then your wish won't come true. Has it spoilt your day?'

Nigel looked deliberately crestfallen and asked plaintively if he could have another go.

She shook her head. 'Sorry, only kids to that. Oh—there it is, see?' She levered it from a leaf with a twig. 'There you are, now your wish will come true. Happy?'

His eyes were warm and tender as they gazed down at her. 'I hope so. Aren't you going to wish?'

Oh yes, she had wished from the bottom of heart that this might be the first of many such outings. She was thankful you couldn't tell your wish.

'Yes, my pin has gone right down there.'

She wondered what he had wished for so feverently when surely he had everything he could possibly want.

Then she felt his arm around her shoulders and she turned to him expectantly, but he was glancing at his watch on his other wrist.

'Look, Emma, we could pop in to a pub and have a snack if you fancy it, but then I'll have to get back. Do you know somewhere decent?'

'I can't say I do, but they're mostly quite good, I believe. I'm not sure if they all do snacks, though.'

They found a pub not far away and had a ploughman's lunch.

'I take it you won't want to be getting back to St Joseph's yet, so I shall I drop you at your home?' Nigel asked as they were leaving the pub.

'Thanks, that would fine,' Emma replied, wishing he could stay longer. Maybe that should have been what she wished at the Well.

'How will you get to St Joseph's? Is there a bus service?'

'Of a sort. But my father will run me back, I expect.'

'Good. Now which way do I go from here?'

It took only a few minutes to drive to her house, and she wondered why he had to hurry back on a Sunday afternoon. Surely whatever he needed to do could wait, and probably would if he had been enjoying himself as she was. The car stopped and she undid her belt reluctantly. She turned to him.

'Thank you so much for a lovely morning. I hope you enjoyed it too.'

Nigel's eyes sparkled with laughter and he leaned towards her and kissed her lightly on the cheek.

'I will have done if my wish comes true,' he replied, and opened the door for her.

She did not watch him drive away in case her mother should be peeping from the window. Instead she ran up the steps to the front door as if she was eager to get indoors.

Her mother could well have been watching, for she opened the door before Emma could.

'Emma!' she cried happily. 'You didn't say you'd be coming home today, and now we've had our dinner. But I can easily get you something.'

'I got a lift here—I didn't know I'd be coming—and we stopped for a ploughman's so I don't need anything else thanks. Where is everybody?'

'Wendy's gone over to Shirley's house and your father is at the golf club, but they'll both be back for tea. So how are you liking the new hospital? Oh, who gave you a lift?'

'Just one of the doctors,' Emma said evasively.

'A doctor? Is he nice?'

'Now, Mum!' Emma protested.

'Well, I'm interested. I don't suppose you'd like it if I wasn't.'

'Of course not. Tell me, have you seen or heard anything of Derek?'

Her mother looked thoughtful. 'Come to think of it, I haven't seen him for some time. He's usually standing in the shop doorway smiling at everyone who passes. Haven't you heard from him?'

'No, but then I never did, he always passed on a message through you or Wendy.'

'Well, I wonder what's happened to him?'

Emma shook her head. 'Perhaps he's got the sack—standing in the doorway and smiling at people who pass by isn't going to do much for trade. D'you know, I feel he's never found his niche in the world. He's pleasant and good-looking, but he doesn't seem exactly right for any job.'

'A boy like that would be good at any job,' her mother said loyally. 'I'd employ him any time and be glad to. When you think of what a lot of young men of his age are like?'

'What I mean is that he isn't the muscular type for physical work and he isn't particularly academic. He seems to fall between two stools.'

'He'll get on all right, you'll see. You'd never find a nicer fellow anywhere.'

But Emma was not really thinking of Derek, her mind was on Nigel. She could still feel the touch of his mouth on her cheek. Granted, it had meant no more to him than a handshake—she could tell by the casual way he did it. But it meant a lot to her. Surely when he saw her on the ward in future he would acknowledge her? She would not like to bet on it.

CHAPTER FOURTEEN

EMMA HAD just finished filling in the chart for a new admission when Sister Borlase beckoned to her from the ward door.

'Thank you, Mr Blake, I think I've got all I need for the time being. Are you quite comfortable? Good, then I'll see you later.' She went to join the Sister.

'Ah, Emma, a patient is being sent up from Casualty, if you'll——'

'Sorry, Sister, but we haven't got a spare bed now. We admitted Mr Blake this morning.' Emma looked anxiously around the ward.

'Yes, I know. This patient will be using the side-ward, if you'll get that ready, please.'

'Very well, Sister. What's his trouble?'

'Both his legs are fractured and possibly his ribs too.'

'Goodness! Did he have an argument with his wife?'

Sister Borlase smiled. 'I don't think he's got one. It's Will Blewett, he's a well-known artist in these parts.'

'I should have thought that was the least dangerous occupation. Was it an RTA?'

'No. Apparently he was painting on the cliffs at Kynance when he stepped back and over the edge and fell on the rocks below.'

Emma looked at her wide-eyed. 'Gosh! That was dreadful. he could easily have been killed. Or drowned, I suppose, if the tide had been in.'

'That depends: If he'd fallen in the sea I should have thought it would have lessened his impact on the rocks.'

'Anyway, he's lucky to be alive. How did he get back up the cliffside? He couldn't have climbed them with

156

those injuries.'

'No, that's where he had a stroke of luck. There was a man fishing nearby and he saw it happen. He'd been going to pack up and leave ten minutes before, but he felt a tug on his rod and decided to hang on in the hope of a catch. Apparently there was nobody else about.'

'Now that was pure luck. I bet the local newspaper will head the story 'Man saved by Fish.'

Sister Borlase laughed. 'And the irony of it is the man didn't get his fish after all that, he was too busy getting help for Will.'

They were laughing when Nigel came into the ward.

'That's good to see, the nursing staff having a ball. Can I share the fun?' he asked, his eyes on Emma.

She gave him a cheeky smile. 'I daresay Sister will tell you all about it. I have work to do.'

'That sounds uncommonly like insubordination, Staff,' Nigel said, and winked as she passed.

The side-ward was small but well equipped with a wash-basin, yet it was not popular with most men patients, who generally preferred to be in the company of others. Emma had just made up the bed when the trolley arrived. A bearded man with tired light blue eyes like some Biblical character lay on the stretcher. The porter handed Emma his notes.

'Will Blewett from Casualty,' he said.

Emma checked that the notes were this patient's, thanked the porter and helped him and the accompanying nurse to transfer him to bed.

When they had gone Emma said, 'Hello, Mr Blewett, 'I'm Staff Nurse Glover. So you've been knocking yourself about a bit?'

'True, dear lady,' he replied hoarsely.

'How did you come to step over the cliff edge? You must know the area pretty well, I hear you often go there painting.'

'A silly answer to a silly question, Nurse. I was nearer

the edge than I realised.'

'Are you sure hadn't had a drink or two?' she said jokingly.

He turned his tired eyes on her. 'Now that, dear lady, is a distinct possibility.' He spoke the words too carefully and Emma guessed she was right.

'Well, no more drinks while you're in my care, Mr Blewett,' she warned him.

'No more drinks? But I may be in here for weeks!' he protested.

'That's more than likely,' she smiled.

'You can't do this to me! I come in here in all good faith like a herring and would go out like a kipper, flat and dehydrated,' he mourned.

'A few glasses of water a day will see that doesn't happen.'

'Water? water? You mean that revolting liquid intended only for ablutions?'

'The same. Known in the trade as Adam's ale.'

'Then Adam is welcome to it. I prefer Will's whiskey.'

'So you're an artist, Mr Blewett?'

'I paint, dear lady, and have been known to write the odd ode.'

'A man of many talents!'

As Emma chatted she was taking his blood pressure and temperature and entering her readings on his chart. She looked towards the door as Nigel came in.

'Ah, Mr Blewett, I'm Dr Shaw, in charge of your case. So you've had a fall. How do you feel?'

'Foul.' Mr Blewett moved his head restlessly from side to side.

'I'm not surprised. Have you been given anything for the pain?'

'No,' he muttered.

Nigel laid a reassuring hand on his shoulder. 'We'll do something about that, old man.' He turned to

Emma. 'Can I have his chart, please? I'll prescribe a pain-killer.'

Emma drew him aside. 'Mr Blewett had been drinking quite heavily, Doctor.'

Nigel looked at her sharply. 'Are you sure?'

She nodded. 'He more or less admitted it.'

He went over to Will Blewett and made some checks, then returned to Emma.

'Thank you, Nurse, we'll have to let him sweat it out for the time being.'

They left the room together. 'How are you liking it here, Emma?' added Nigel.'

'Very much indeed, especially now I've got used to it.'

'And now you're a staff nurse. How does that feel?'

'Wonderful,' she said. She could have given him two reasons for that. One was that she was no longer being constantly put down by Sister Darling and the other was that she could speak to him when she was on duty. But she would not have told him either reason.

She returned to the main ward to attend other patients and enjoyed every minute because she and Nigel were now on friendly terms, something she had never thought could happen.

As the days passed Will Blewett showed much skill as an artist. He was seldom without a pencil and pad in his hand and drew everything he could see and many things he couldn't.

Emma was taking his blood pressure one morning when he reached up and took a long chestnut hair from her shoulder and examioned it.

'Fair tresses Man's imperial race ensnare.

And beauty draws us with a single hair,' he said theatrically.

'Sorry about the hair. Did you write that?' asked Emma, thinking that it sounded profound, but she had no idea what it meant.

'I, dear lady? Indeed no. It was penned by one Alexander Pope some two hundred years ago. One wonders what he might have written could he have seen the colour of your hair.'

Emma was now accustomed to his flowery language. She knew nothing of the quality of his odes; those he had recited seemed senseless, but his sketches were excellent.

'I'd love to see some of your real pictures,' she said.

'And so you shall, my dear lady, when I have left this arena of sickness. Will I be here much longer?'

'I shouldn't think so, but you'll have to wait until the doctor says you're fit to be discharged. You'll be on crutches for a time,' she warned.

'Crutches won't bother me so long as I have a hand with which to wield my brush. I'll speak to the doctor today.'

'It will be up to Dr Shaw when you can leave, and he's away for a few days.'

As she left him she thought of Nigel, who had told her he was going to London, and asked if she had any messages for anyone at Nightingale's. Nightingale's! So he would be seeing Sister Darling. He had looked down at her, a question in his long-lashed eyes.

'Message? Oh, I don't think so. Everyone I knew left when I did. Oh—except for Staff Nurse Bishop, I shared a flat with her.'

Nigel raised his eyebrows. 'And the message?'

She stared at him blankly. 'Just "Hi," I suppose.'

'Hardly worth while to search her out for that, I think. Nothing else? No news? No intimation as to whether you're happy here, hm?'

Emma frowned. 'I'll drop her a line some time.'

Then he had gone, and she wondered when he would be back, and she was deeply envious of Sister Darling.

Emma was making Will's bed when he reached up

and with uncanny dexterity drew out the pins securing her hair. It fell in a cascade around her shoulders and she drew back in dismay.

'Mr Blewett, you'll get me the sack!' She tried to find the pins, but he held them aloft in one hand. 'Please give them to me.' She looked anxiously towards the door.

'Soon, I must study it for one moment.'

She was on tenderhooks as he arranged her hair as he wanted it, but she decided it would be quicker to allow him to get on with it than struggle for the pins. He examined it from the roots to tips, noticing the rippling way it fell, then almost absentmindedly handed her back the pins.

'Many thanks, dear lady,' he said, and reached for his pencil and pad.

When Emma was off duty she went to the Refectory for a poached egg on toast. Nurse Matthews beckoned her across.

'Nice to have a bit of company,' she smiled. 'How's Will doing?'

'Will? You mean Will Blewett? D'you know him?'

'Know him? Everybody does,' Karen laughed. 'He usually spends Sunday mornings in the local and leaves very unsteadily when it closes to go back to his studio and paint lovely pictures.'

Emma looked thoughtful. 'So he drinks a lot?'

'He lives on the stuff!'

'Now when he was admitted he grumbled about having to do without his whisky, and he hasn't mentioned it since. I thought it was his exaggerated way of talking, but I wonder. He's had several jolly-looking visitors.' The girls stared at each other. 'I guess I'd better search his locker.'

'Won't he be leaving soom? He's been in quite a while.'

'Yes, any day now. Are you thinking what I think you

are?'

Karen nodded. 'If he's getting on all right and he's happy, what's the point of spoiling his last few days.'

'I don't think we've had this conversation, have we?' Emma looked doubtful.

Karen chuckled. 'I remember being in the pub one morning having a pasty when he stood swaying in the doorway reciting his rubbishy poetry and flinging out his arms in theatrical gestures when he accidentally knocked the drink out of a visitor's hand.'

'What happened?'

'Simon, the landlord, said "Now then, Will, off you go, you're not welcome here this morning. But first of all you pay for that drink."'

'And did he?'

'I don't think he understood, but Simon took the money from his pockets. As he fiddled around to find it Will flung his arms around him and giggled and said, "Darling, I didn't know you cared." We were all convulsed, and sorry when he staggered out.'

'He's certainly a character. He's always drawing and his sketches seem very good to my untrained eye, but I'd really like to see his real pictures.'

'He has an exhibition in Newlyn Art Gallery every so often, and he must be pretty well off. Or could be if he didn't spend it on booze.'

'Do let me know next time there's an exhibiton, won't you?' asked Emma.

'I won't need to do that, it's plastered all over the place because his work is popular. I must get back. Are you off now?'

When Emma reached the hostel she glanced at the pigeonholes automatically, although she seldom received letters now she was able to get home more often. But today she saw she had one. She looked at the envelope curiously, not recognising the writing. Could it be from Dorothy? She waited until she was in her room and settled down in a chair which was much more comfortable than those in her room in the Mile End flat, before tearing it open. There was only one sheet of notepaper, and glancing down it she saw it was from Derek. She was pleased because she'd been worried about him.

'Dear Emma' it began in large, childish writing, 'I've been away so I haven't been in touch, but now I'm back and longing to see you, because I've got something very special to say. I want to take you out to dinner to the Penberthy Castle Hotel! It's very posh and pricey, I know, but this is a very special occasion. Could you make it Friday? If you ring the shop it would be best and they'll pass on the message, Love Derek.'

Emma smiled happily as she replaced it in its envelope. Dear Derek, she wondered what his something special was—something pretty special for sure, because that hotel would set him back a bit. But that was Derek, pay now and probably repay his mother later. She smiled at the bit about ringing the shop. He was on the phone at home, but his mother, despite her red knickers, gave the impression that she would disapprove of any girlfriend Derek had.

The Penberthy Castle was well known in the district as being exceedingly up-market and was patronised by wealthy visitors or local yuppies out to impress. Emma giggled. Did Derek picture himself as a Yuppie now he had a sports car? She had never been inside the hotel, but the father of one of her school friends was a violinist in the small string band which played there in the evenings. It would be great to pass those elegant doors, and she would have to try not to worry about how much it would be costing Derek.

Fortunately she had the dress she had bought for the party, but it was at home. If she told Derek she was free on Friday it would be useful, because she could go home first and he could pick her up there. She would ring his shop in the morning.

CHAPTER FIFTEEN

WHEN EMMA rang the shop the manager replied and seemed disinclined to call Derek.

'Can I give him a message?' he asked grudgingly.

'Yes, please, if you'll tell him I'll expect him to call for me at home at seven-fifteen on Friday,' Emma said.

'Seven-fifteen Friday at your home?'

'Thank you, yes.'

The manager grunted and replaced the receiver. Emma felt a momentary sadness for Derek having to work there with a manager who was clearly not very friendly.

By Friday Emma had thought more and more about Derek and the something special he had to tell her. She wondered what it could be, and with a jolt of dismay hoped he would not want to borrow money for one of his ambitions, a more expensive car, a holiday abroad. She thought of her meagre savings with fierce protectiveness. It had been difficult enough to save and she certainly did not want it frittered away. Derek was always so boyishly enthusiastic it could be difficult to refuse him. Maybe he was thinking of changing his job, but it did not seem very likely, because darling though he was, he had no skills to offer. Oh well, she would soon find out what it was.

Emma put on her green and white dress and decided not to plait her hair, it made her look too much like a schoolgirl which was all right when she was a student, but now she was a staff nurse. She tied it back with the green satin ribbon and was pleased with the result. She fastened some chunky green beads round her neck, put on some green eye-shadow, sprayed on her expensive perfume which so far had not fulfilled the TV commercial claims for it—no man had swooned at her approach. Maybe she did not get such a bargain buying it from that stall in the market.

When she went downstairs her mother was full of admiration and smiled proudly.

'You'll make a lovely looking couple,' she said.

'Couple? There's only one of me. You've been at the bottle,' Emma joked.

'Silly! I mean you and Derek of course. I couldn't be more pleased.'

'Dismayed amazement flooded through Emma. Surely—oh, heavens, oh no! She had not time to worry about it now, because the bell rang and Derek had arrived.

'Bring Derek in,' her mother cried fondly.

'Sorry, must rush. Cheerio.' Emma fled.

But now the evening was tinged with an awful fear. Oh God, if he had it in his mind to propose to her what on earth was she going to say? She had a brief feeling of relief when she saw he was not dressed in his sports car gear, although now, with this other thing on her mind, it seemed of minimal importance. Actually he looked very smart and good-looking in a dark suit, white shirt and neat tie. His eyes were shining as if he were about to burst with excitement. All the same, he looked at Emma admiringly.

'You look great. No matter how dolled-up the other women at the Penberth Castle may be, I've got the best one.'

She wanted to cry out, 'But you haven't got me'. She wished she could be back on duty, but all the same, she knew she could not spoil his evening.

'You look very smart, and your car is even nicer than I remembered.'

'Do you think so? I'm really delighted with it, it

seems to have changed my life. Anything seems possible now. Normally I wouldn't have bought a new suit for tonight. Come to think of it, I would never have dreamed of coming to the Penberth Castle either. But what's money for?'

'I suppose it's to buy the things you want. Only it's wise to have some put by.'

Derek looked triumphant. 'I would have thought the same once, but now I believe in getting what you want and paying later.'

'It can be the road to disaster.' Emma felt a hundred years older than him.

'Not necessarily. If a new suit and a dinner at a posh hotel with your girl can give you happiness now what would be the use of of waiting until later on when you might not want it?'

'Maybe you're right.' Emma did not feel in the mood to argue.

'Can you guess what I'm going to tell you?' he asked, driving faster than he should.

She glanced at the speedometer. 'You'll get nicked if you drive like that, and it'll spoil our evening,' she warned him, glad to change the subject.

Derek gave a guilty laugh. 'Thanks for reminding me—this car goes faster than I realise. It must be fantastic to drive at Brands Hatch. Maybe one day——' he said dreamily.

Emma suppressed a sigh. Derek and his desires could become tedious. Would he never be content?

However, she had successfully stopped him from telling her what it was they were going to celebrate, and she was relieved, for the longer she put it off the better. She did so want him to enjoy this evening which was obviously giving him so much pleasure.

The hotel was set on a hill in a tree-lined garden. Lights shone from the many windows and in the car park there were very expensive cars.

Derek proudly parked his TR7. 'It can hold its own with any of them, can't it?' he said, peering at a minute mark on the bonnet.

As Emma was getting out a button on her coat accidentally caught the corner of a cloth in the door's pocket. She stopped to pick it up and saw it was indeed a pair of red knickers.

She held them up and said jokingly, 'Who's the girlfriend?'

Derek looked taken aback and was about to deny the remark when he saw what she was holding.

'Oh no, it's my polishing cloth. I got it from Mum's duster cupboard because it matches my car.'

'Pull the other one,' Emma teased.

'No, really. You're the only girl I've ever taken out in the car.'

The dining room was well patronised and the small orchestra on a dais at one end of the room played softly and pleasantly and was suitable for the mainly middle-aged clientele. They were shown a table in the centre of the room by the aisle, and Emma would have preferred to be against a wall or window, but she had no intention of letting Derek think she was not pleased with the arrangement.

He looked around uncertainly until they were handed outsize menus.

'I'd thought we'd have a drink before, but—well——'

'Never mind, I'm sure we'll enjoy the meal without it. There's a fantastic choice, isn't there?'

As they studied what was on offer Emma tried not to notice the prices. Then the waiter presented them with the wine list, and her heart sank, because she did see those prices.

Derek looked excited. 'We're going to do it properly, we'll have a bottle of wine.'

'We could have half a bottle, that should be enough,' she said.

Derek shook his head. 'No, this is a very special occasion.' Her heart felt paralysed. Whatever happened she must stop him from telling her what it was he had to say until the meal was over.

She asked him, fruitlessly, what he thought some of the foreign-sounding dishes might be. He had no idea, and Emma kept up a frantic, hysterical conversation on what they might be, afraid to allow silence to descend.

When they had ordered Derek leaned forward, his eyes shining.

'Emma,' he began.

'Oh, what's that tune they're playing?' she interrupted.

He looked puzzled. 'I've no idea. I know the tune but not the name. What I was——'

'It's always the way, isn't it? I don't know how people in the TV programme 'Name that Tune' can remember so many, do you?'

He shook his head, 'I don't think I know the programme. What I was going——'

'Which programmes do you like?'

She saw their meal arrive and heaved a sigh of relief. 'Doesn't it look lovely? And it says all the vegetables are home-grown. They always taste different from the frozen ones, don't they? Shall I put some on your plate, or would you rather help yourself?'

She could hear herself talking incessantly, and anyone who happened to overhear her must be wondering how the nice-looking young man could tolerate her. But it wouldn't be much longer before they finished this meal which was giving him so much pleasure.

At last even Derek got fed up with her chatter and laid down his knife and fork and put his hand over hers. 'Hold on, Emma, I brought you here to say something very important and you aren't giving me the chance. I know you're excited.'

Her heart spiralled down inside her. Now it was

inevitable he would speak.

'So you have Derek—I'm sorry. Do tell me.'

The excitement reappeared in his eyes. 'You know I said that one day I'd go to America?'

'You don't mean you're going there?' she asked in amazement.

He shook his head. 'Not exactly. Not yet. But—' his face lit up wit delight, 'but I've got a promotion and I'm moving to the main shop in Bristol. I've been on a management course, so, I'm on my way up, aren't I?'

'Congratulations, Derek, that's marvellous! But what has Bristol got to do with America?'

'Don't you see? Bristol—perhaps London, then America. The sky's the limit now I'm on the up and up.'

Emma held her breath. Was it now? Was he going to ask her now. But apparently he had said what he wanted, and now he picked up his knife and fork and continued eating.

Emma experienced the most wonderful feeling of relief, as if a heavy-weight had fallen from her. In an exuberence of affection for him she leaned forward implulsively and kissed the tip of his nose.

'You're sweet—it's wonderful news,' she said with a delighted smile.

She glanced up at a passing couple and her smile disappeared as if it had been wiped away, for incredibly she found she was looking into Nigel's impassive face. She must be hallucinating. She glanced at his companion and she had made no mistake, for Sister Darling, dressed to kill, was with him. He smiled, then glancing at Derek gave him a friendly wink as he passed by and murmured, 'Bon appétit.'

There was no way Nigel could have missed seeing the kiss she had given Derek, and embarrassment gripped her like a vice. Nevertheless she was still feeling the euphoria of relief. Yet stronger than those two emotions was another, and it was jealousy. Recently Nigel had been so friendly to her she had almost put Sister Darling out of her mind. Apparently he had not, because he had been to London and brought her back with him. She would have liked to observe them, but she would have to turn around to do so. Sister Darling had looked very smart as she passed in a backless dress with no wrap, so presumably she was staying in the hotel.

Derek was talking, telling her of his aims, and surely Bristol had never before been mentioned so much. He must have read the history of it from time immemorial and knew the name and site of ever place of interest and was determined she should know just where they were, drawing diagrams of the area with a spoon on the tablecloth. Emma wore an interested smile and made what she hoped were appropriate remarks, but only a small part of her mind was so occupied. The rest of the evening seemed endless, but at last it was over. She struggled to the end to match Derek's delight and enthusiasm and to thank him for a lovely evening as they said goodbye on the doorstep. She waited by the front door until he drove away, then went indoors feeling near exhaustion and glad to get into bed.

She could not sleep, for despite her relief over Derek's news she felt flat and puzzled. The last thing she had wanted was for him to propose to her, but she could not help wondering why he had never even kissed her. They got on well together, and she was the girl he took to discos and out in his precious car, and to dinner to hear his news. She searched her mind for reason, and came up with the plain fact that he found her physically unattractive, and the knowledge hurt. She felt very alone and unwanted. Derek was going away and it was no use thinking of Nigel. She had got on well with him too, but it could have meant nothing. She wondered what it was she lacked—obviously something Sister Darling had. Was it sophistication? Brains. Those things did not make a person physically attractive.

Emma shook her head and sighed. Whatever it was she had not got it, so what did the future hold for her? She reached for a tissue and blew her nose. She would devote her life to her career, go to university, take a course in administration. Then she remembered that Sister Darling was already in that. A tear trickled into her pillow. That woman had got everything.

CHAPTER SIXTEEN

EMMA WAS leaving Will Blewett's room when she saw Nigel walking along the corridor, and she tensed as she waited for him to reach her. If only he did not look so attractive, life would be easier.

'Good morning, Staff. I take it you want to speak to me?' He was standing too close for her peace of mind, and as she looked down she could see the bib of her apron moving to and fro with the fierce beating of her heart.

'Yes, Doctor. Mr Blewett is anxious to be discharged, and—I've been telling him he must wait for your return.'

He thought for a moment. 'Mr Blewett. Oh yes, he was going to be fitted with crutches by Physio. How is he coping?' He raised an eyebrow questioningly.

'Very well. He was given them three days ago.'

'Right. Then I'll have a word with him later.' He gave her a nod and started to walk when he turned back. 'Oh—congratulations.'

'Emma looked up in surprise and saw an enigmatic expression in his long-lashed eyes.

'Congratulations? What for?'

'Last night—didn't I arrive at a very special moment?' Nigel tipped up her left hand lightly and glanced down at it.

She felt again the embarrassment she had experienced last night and shook her head vigorously. 'Yes—but not for me, it was because——'

Her words were lost as Nigel spoke over them. 'You would hardly kiss your young man in full view of everybody in a hotel dining room unless you were celebrating something very important. Isn't that so?'

'But it wasn't important to me,' she protested, the colour rising in her cheeks.

'No?' There was a mocking look in his eyes. 'Then tell James Hunt from me it's time he got out of first gear or he might get pipped at the post.'

'But you've got it all wrong. It was because he was going . . .' Her words trailed away, and she need not have attempted to contradict him, for he had already moved away to join Sister Borlase, who had got out of the lift.

Emma sank her teeth into her lip, feeling furious with him, with Derek and herself. He might have had the decency to listen to her explanation, and would have done had he been interested. But it was not fair that he could say what he liked then walk away. He was beastly! But after a few minutes she felt differently. She was glad he had thought Derek had proposed to her, anything was better than letting him believe she was not attractive to anybody. No doubt he felt very smug knowing he had Sister Darling, so let him think she had Derek!

She went to the ward to allow Nurse Matthews to go for coffee. Most of the men were sitting beside their beds wearing striped pyjamas, dark dressing-gowns and slippers. Some were reading newspapers, others were talking to each other, while a few stared into space, no doubt thinking of home. Undoubtedly they all had someone who loved them and thought them special. Emma sighed.

When she returned to Will Blewett's room he was

sketching as usual.

'Has the doctor given you your marching orders?' she asked.

He rested his bleary eyes on her. 'Alas, Emma he hasn't yet graced this miserable room with his presence, but I can wait, because it means I'm able to refresh my memory of you.'

Emma laughed. 'I should have thought you'd be glad to see the last of me. You probably are, but you're too polite to say so.'

He indicated a chair by the window with a gesture. 'Sit over there, if you will, and look towards the window.'

'Will, I can't waste time here, you seem determined to get me the sack!'

'It's imperative I see your jawline, I haven't got it quite right.'

'Are you sketching me?'

'I am indeed. Would I turn my back on such an opportunity?'

Emma sat as he had requested. 'OK? Then I demand a model's fee!'

'He sketched in silence, then put his pad aside and thanked her.

'May I see it?' She walked over to him.

He shook his head. 'There's nothing for you to see, nothing you would recognise.'

'It isn't fair, you can't draw me behind my back,' she said, laughing at the absurdity of her remark.

'You shall see it when it's completed and framed. I'll exhibit it in the Newlyn Art Gallery when it's finished.'

'You've got a nerve, using me as a model without asking my permission.' Emma joked.

'Do I ask a seagull's permission when it's flying over

the cliffs?'

'And look what happened to you when you were painting that!'

'A cautionary tale,' Will agreed. 'One day I'll recompense you. Or is it reward enough to see how beautiful you are?'

The door opened, and Nigel came in and looked from one laughing face to the other. He raised his eyebrows and murmured to Emma. 'You're boyfriend may be in first gear, but you certainly are not .' Then, raising his voice, he said, 'I hear you're anxious to leave us, Mr Blewett.'

Will looked at him with watery eyes. 'Would that I might take with me this damsel with the nut-brown hair but alas. I am unable. The restrictions of hospital life fill me with despair, so yes, I would like to bid you farewell.'

Nigel nodded. 'I've seen your X-rays and read your notes. The bones are knitting together nicely and you're in good shape health-wise, so I see no reason to keep you any longer.' He crossed to the window, looked out for a moment, then turned, one hand in his pocket. 'When you were first brought in you believed you couldn't manage without your "wee dram", didn't you? But you have, and it's done you nothing but good.'

Emma thought how pompous and self-satisfied he sounded and choked back a laugh as she and Will exchanged a glance.

Will flung out an arm in a theatrical gesture. ''I presented myself at Betty's bedside late at night with considerably liquor concealed about my person.'' One of my favourite quotations. Are you acquainted with it, sir?'

Nigel gave him a searching look. 'I hope you don't

mean what I think, but I'm afraid you probably do. You would do well to leave here today before I change my mind. And you'd better beware. We don't want you falling over cliffs again, you might not come off so fortunately another time.' He gave a stiff nod and left hurriedly. While he thinks he's on the winning side, Emma thought nastily.

Later in the day Will's jolly-looking friend called for him and handed him a bottle which he passed to Emma.

'What's this?' she asked.

'A small gift for my angel of mercy.'

She tore back the paper and saw it was a bottle of sherry.

'I can't take this, Will, but thanks all the same, I'm sure you'll make good use of it,' she said, touched by his unexpected generosity.

He pushed towards her again. 'A small fee for your modelling services.' He pulled himself to his feet, adjusted his crutches and turning to her, bowed his head so that his beard rested on his shirt front. 'I hope I may see you again, Emma my love.' Then he made his way from the room with dexterous speed.

Life seemed dull now that Will had left, and Emma also missed having Derek somewhere in the background. Worst of all was having to keep her distance from Nigel, knowing, that he was committed to Sister Darling. She realised it could be just as lonely as it had been in London, and it was with a feeling of pleasure that she recieved a letter from Dorothy, and she settled down to read it.

'Hello kid, and how's the Wild West? Teeming with cream and Cornish pasties? I saw Dr Shaw the other day. As he passed me he said "Hi", which surprised me greatly. Wasn't like him, was it? It's great being Staff here, I bully all the students, you may be sure. Had a card from Celia in Malawi, but no news, I don't know why she bothered. Heather is in your room and a bossy girl called Sharon, from Birmingham, is in Celia's. I think she's got the message that she can't be bossy with me, I've lived through it all. Talking about being bossy, Pamela Darling is lording it over Admin. Half of us think she'll take over from the SNO when she goes, but the other half say she's got other ideas. News! She and Dr Shaw went away together, what d'you think of that? Wedding bells? Or don't they bother with those any more? I bet you envy her, don't you? Keep in touch, Dorothy.'

Emma rested her chin in her hands and stared into space. Dorothy had the unfailing knack of always saying what you didn't want to hear. She knew Sister Darling and Nigel had gone away together, because he had brought her down here, but to have had it reported just underlined it and made it harder to bear. Dorothy was daft! Why should she imagine she would envy Sister Darling? Nigel was nothing to her. Nothing at all, she repeated as she tore up the letter and put the pieces in the waste-paper basket.

She felt she had to get away from her thoughts, so she decided to go out to the town. Normally she would have gone home for the weekend, but now that Derek was not available there was nothing to go there for. She could not go to the disco alone. But she was not going to let that stop her enjoying herself. She would go to the shops, have tea there, buy some chocolates to eat in front of the TV this evening. What did it matter if she put on weight?

There would undoubtedly be a long wait for the infrequent bus, so she decided to walk to town across the downs. It was quiet and peaceful, the sky was blue and seagulls cried and swooped overhead. Everywhere looked so beautiful with the purple heather and yellow gorse and the blue sea in the distance that her spirits rose.

She thought of Will and wondered how her portrait had turned out. She was looking forward to seeing it, for already notices advertised the exhibition. She wondered, too, about Derek and how he was faring in Bristol. She doubted if she would ever hear as he was no letter-writer. And even if she saw his mother she would not ask her because of her withdrawn, unfriendly expression. Moreover, she knew that for evermore she would picture her in red knickers, a forbidding hat and gloves. Her thoughts, all the time, tried to focus on Nigel, but she did not allow them to do so.

It was a long walk, but enjoyable. Nevertheless when Emma reached the town her first desire was to go in the café and sit down by the window to watch the shoppers. She ordered splits and cream saffron buns with reckless disregard for her figure. It was so long since she had been able to indulge in them. She had been away from Cornwall for so long that whereas in the past she had been sure to see someone passing who she knew. Now they were all strangers. Even at the thought her heart jumped, for she recognised the tall fair-haired man on the opposite pavement. He stood out from the others, taller and more handsome. Might he—was it possible he might come in here? He paused for a moment, then disappeared into a shop. Emma leaned forward to see which shop it was and with a sinking feeling saw it was a

jeweller's. It made sense. He would be buying an
engagement ring. It had been on the cards for a long
time, but now it was confirmed. She wished, after all,
she had not eaten this tea, she felt quite sick. All desire
for chocolates to eat this evening had left her. There was
nothing she wanted in the shops, so she paid her bill and
left to stand at the bus stop. As time went on she sat on
the nearby fence without bothering to look at the
timetable. She was in no hurry to return.

After some time she saw Nigel's Porsche approaching
and looked the other way. The last thing she wanted was
to be given a lift by him, but it was a long time before
the bus would arrive.

The next time she had an afternoon off it was the day
of the Art Exhibition, and she set off for Newlyn full of
curiosity. What sort of a picture had Will done of her?
She hoped he would have made her look neat and tidy,
but knowing his peculiar mind she would not put it past
him to have painted her with untidy wisps of hair falling
down from her cap, a creased apron and quite possibly
holding a bedpan, so it was with some trepidation that
she paid her entrance fee and received a catalogue.

Pictures by many local artists covered the walls, and
Emma purposely did not read the catalogue to see where
Will's would be. She preferred to come upon them
unexpectedly. As she looked at the excellent seascapes,
landscapes, still-lifes and portaits she realised it was
quite possible Will's had not been hung, but she hoped
it had, for his sake as well as her own. She joined a
group of people to see the picture they were admiring,
and her heart leapt. There were exclamations of praise
from everybody, and it was indeed beautiful. It showed
the head and shoulders of a girl dressed in green, but it
was a pale green and the colour which dominated the
picture was the colour of the hair, a rich chestnut brown

which hung down in an undulating shawl. Each hair seemed separate and colourful, and Emma looked at the face, a pale oval with pink cheeks and huge sad brown eyes. Surely she did not look like that? Somebody touched her shoulder and she swung around.

'Nigel!' The name came from her unbidden. 'It—it's a good picture isn't it? I had no idea Will was so talented.'

He smiled at her. 'It's almost as good as the original.'

She laughed in embarrassment. 'It flatters me, but of course I never actually sat for him, he just did sketches of me when I was in his room.'

'It's an excellent likeness.'

'Is it? I'm sure I've never looked so sad.'

'Do you see what he's called it?' He pointed to an entry in the catalogue: Emma in Love.

She looked up at him in amazement. I wonder what gave him that idea? I've never been in love.'

She felt the pressure of his hand on her shoulder. 'No?'

'No, honestly.' She looked up wide-eyed, but when she saw the look on his face her gaze faltered and she looked away.

'I'd like to buy it,' Nigel said presently.

'*You* would? But——' She thought of Sister Darling's reaction if he did and she had to hang it on their wall.

'But what?' he prompted.

'It—it might not be wise, if you get married.'

He raised his eyebrows. 'Why not?'

'Well, no wife would want another girl's portrait on the wall, now would she? You must realise that.'

'Maybe not, but I'll risk it. Come over to the desk with me and they'll see why I want it.'

Emma accompanied him reluctantly. She did not

want her picture to hang on their wall like a peeping Tom to witness their happiness. She knew, too, that Sister Darling would make disparaging remarks about it. She turned to look at it again, and saw with relief that it had green disc on the corner. 'It means it isn't for sale,' she said thankfully.

'Every man has his price, and I don't imagine I'll have difficulty in persuading Mr Blewett to part with it.' Nigel said confidently.

'But—but I might want to buy it myself,' she protested.

'Do you?'

She did not know what to reply, but felt she would do anything to prevent Sister Darling getting it. But Nigel—if he really wanted it——maybe he would hang it in his room in the hospital.

She looked up at him, a feeling of hopeless love in her heart. Could she refuse him anything?

'Well, do you?' he asked again.

She hung her head. 'If you had it would you hang it in your room at the hospital?'

'So that everybody would see it and recognise you as Emma in Love?'

She saw the sardonic look in his eyes and shook her head. 'Oh no, of course you couldn't do that, or they'd wonder why you put it there.'

He gazed at her so tenderly she longed to stay there in the warmth of his smile for ever. 'I think they might guess,' he said softly.

'Don't be silly,' she said, and turned away, her eyes damp with unshed tears.

'Am I silly, Emma?' His voice was gentle and tender, and she could hardly bear it.

He was deliberately torturing her, and she made a sudden move away from him. She was not going to stay there and let him say what he liked.

His voice and manner changed. 'There's the artist,' he said, and steered her towards him. 'Ah, Mr Blewett,' he said affably. 'You're managing well on your crutches, I see.'

Will turned to him carefully. 'I'm not managing at all well, sir. I can get around with difficulty, that's all.' His voice was slurred.

'Give it time, it's early days. I've been admiring your work, especially the girl in green, and I'd like to buy it.'

'NFS sir.' Will turned away and caught sight of Emma, who was hanging back. 'Ah, the nut-brown maiden herself. And are you pleased with your likeness, dear lady?'

'It's wonderful, Will, really lovely. But you're very naughty, you've flattered me, you know.'

Will shook his head. 'It's a likeness, I don't dabble in flattery.' He turned to Nigel. 'Do you agree, sir, it's a likeness?'

'I do indeed,' Nigel said, 'and that's why I want to buy it. So name your price, old man.'

Will threw back his head so that his beard jutted forward antagonistically. 'I repeat, sir, it's not for sale to an outsider.'

Emma glanced at Nigel and to her surprise felt sorry for him. She guessed it must be the first time in his life he had been referred to as an outsider. But she was delighted to think Sister Darling would not have it.

'The picture is for Emma—not yet—but when the time comes I'll present it to her as a wedding gift. Her husband will undoubtedly appreciate it. In the meantime it will remain in my studio.' Will inclined his head and turned aside, and was immediately surrounded by friends and admirers.

Nigel stood for a few more minutes staring at the picture, then, taking Emma's arm he steered her out through the crowded room, into the street, and down a lane which led to the sea-front. It was a beautiful afternoon, the sun shone on the rippling water and on the castle which was on top of the Mount. In front of them was the beach, deserted because it was shingle instead of sand. They sat on the low stone wall that looked out to sea. A gentle breeze ruffled her hair.

'It was a beautiful picture,' Nigel said thoughtfully. 'How clever of him to catch the expression on your face.'

'He must have dreamed it up. I never look like that,' Emma laughed.

Nigel's eyes were warm and tender. 'You do, you know. It's how I always think of you.'

Emma felt a wave of anger. What did he think he was playing at, talking in that way? He might enjoy playing this game, but she was not going to join in. She would put a stop to it, once and for all.

'I had a letter from Dorothy Bishop. She tells me everyone at Nightingale's is wondering when Sister Darling is going to announce her engagement.' She forced herself to sound uncaring.

'Really? I didn't know she was getting married.'

Emma scowled up at him. 'You know what hospitals are. If two members of staff go away together they naturally form their own conclusion. They know you brought her down here.'

'Only because her holidays fell when I was returning here and she had long wanted to see Cornwall. I gave her a lift. I seem to remember doing the same for you.'

Emma rose to her feet in disgust. 'I think I'll be getting back now,' she said coldly.

Nigel reached up and pulled her down beside him again.

'Listen to me, Emma. At one time I was very fond of Pamela, but it's all over now and has been for a long time.'

'But I saw you going into a jeweller's shop after she'd been down.'

He absentmindedly pushed his hair back from his forehead. 'I see. And you put two and two together and came up with an engagement ring. You haven't been in a hospital for nothing! Actually, would you believe my visit there had nothing to do with her? I'd taken in some stones I found on the beach to be polished.'

'All the same——'

'You must believe me, Emma. There's nothing between me and Pamela., She's set her mind on becoming the SNO in due course, and admits that domestic life doesn't appeal to her at all.'

'To her surprise Emma felt sorry for him. She hated to think his feelings would have been hurt, that he had been rejected. 'I'm sorry,' she said.'

He shook his head. 'Don't be, it all worked out right.'

'Right?'

Nigel felt for her hand and took it in his. 'A long time ago I fell in love with you, Emma. At times you looked as if you loved me too, because you looked just like Will's portrait and I ached to hold you in my arms. Then young Derek came on the scene with his TR7 and it was hell. He seemed so right for you, and I couldn't break that up. Do you love him, Emma?'

She knew she must be imagining this, but it was a lovely dream. Then his hand was on her arm and he was repeating, 'Do you, Emma?' His voice was so wistful she reached out for him.

'Oh no, Derek has always been a good friend, but no more than that.'

She felt the pressure of his hands on hers. 'Then I can tell you I love you, Emma. And more than anything I want you to marry me. Will you?'

The sun was dazzling and somewhere it seemed bells were ringing. She looked up at Nigel in wonderment. 'Oh, Nigel!'

He drew her close, kissed first one eye and then the other, then his mouth travelled over her cheeks until they reached her throat. She trembled with ecstasy and felt she must cry out, but she was silenced as his lips found hers in a kiss which was tender yet fiercely passionate. When he released her and she felt weak but wonderful.

'I hope your answer was yes, because people were passing, and a nice girl wouldn't kiss a man in public unless there was something special to celebrate, now would she?'

Emma punched him. 'You can't fool me. You only want to marry me so you can have that picture, don't you?'

'But of course. I always get what I want by one means or another. Sometimes,' Nigel added with a smile, 'by throwing a pin in a wishing well.'

'The wishing well! What *did* you wish for that day?'

He planted a kiss on her nose. 'Wouldn't you like to know?'

She opened her mouth to protest. 'I wished for

something like this,' he said softly, his lips possessively over hers.

IS PASSION A CRIME?

Mills & Boon

WINTER

COMPETITION

How would you like a
year's supply of Mills & Boon Romances ABSOLUTELY FREE?
Well, you can win them! All you have to do is complete the word
puzzle below and send it into us by 30th June 1989.
The first five correct entries picked out of the bag after that date
will each win a year's supply of Mills & Boon Romances (Ten
books every month - **worth over £100!**) What could be easier?

C	W	A	E	T	A	N	R	E	B	I	H
H	R	I	C	E	R	W	O	L	G	M	Y
I	F	R	O	S	T	A	O	E	L	U	Y
L	N	I	B	O	R	U	D	R	I	V	Y
L	B	L	E	A	K	B	W	I	I	N	F
T	O	G	L	O	V	E	S	E	A	R	R
S	O	S	G	O	L	R	W	I	E	T	E
T	T	C	H	F	I	R	E	L	R	O	E
S	K	A	T	E	M	Y	C	I	K	S	Z
I	Y	R	R	E	M	I	P	I	N	E	E
N	A	F	D	E	C	E	M	B	E	R	N
N	C	E	M	I	S	T	L	E	T	O	E

Ivy	Radiate	December	Star	Merry
Frost	Chill	Skate	Ski	Pine
Bleak	Glow	Mistletoe	Inn	
Boot	Ice	Fire		
Robin	Hibernate	Log		**PLEASE TURN**
Yule	Icicle	Scarf		**OVER FOR**
Freeze	Gloves	Berry		**DETAILS**
				ON HOW
				TO ENTER

How to enter

All the words listed overleaf, below the word puzzle, are hidden in the grid. You can find them by reading the letters forwards, backwards, up or down, or diagonally. When you find a word, circle it, or put a line through it. After you have found all the words the remaining letters (which you can read from left to right, from the top of the puzzle through to the bottom) will spell a secret message.

Don't forget to fill in your name and address in the space provided and pop this page in an envelope (you don't need a stamp) and post it today. Hurry - competition ends 30th June 1989

Only one entry per household please.

Mills & Boon Competition, FREEPOST, P.O. Box 236, Croydon, Surrey CR9 9EL.

Secret message _____

_____

Name_____

Address_____

_____

_____

_____ Postcode _____